NEWPORT SUMMER

Other books by Nikki Poppen

The Romany Heiress
The Heroic Baron
The Dowager's Wager

NEWPORT SUMMER

•

Nikki Poppen

AVALON BOOKS
NEW YORK

Published by Thomas Bouregy & Co., Inc.
160 Madison Avenue, New York, NY 10016

Library of Congress Cataloging-in-Publication Data

Poppen, Nikki, 1967-
    Newport Summer / Nikki Poppen.
        p.   cm.
    ISBN 978-0-8034-9936-2 (acid-free paper)   1. Nobility—
Great Britain—Fiction   2. Newport (R. I.)—Fiction.   I. Title.

PS3616.O657N49 2009
813'.6—dc22

                                                    2008031624

PRINTED IN THE UNITED STATES OF AMERICA
ON ACID-FREE PAPER
BY HADDON CRAFTSMEN, BLOOMSBURG, PENNSYLVANIA

For my agent, Scott at Greyhaus, and for my great
editor, Faith, who both give me the chance to do
something I love. Thanks so much for all
the opportunities you've provided me.

Chapter One

London, England, May 1887, the drawing room of the Earl of Camberly's town house

"**I**s that all, milord?" Mr. Lawbee, the somberly dressed clerk from Christie's auction house was stiffly polite and not the least bit sarcastic or ingratiating in his tone, although, Lord knew, he could have been.

Gannon Maddox, fourth Earl of Camberly, pushed a hand through his immaculate dark hair and fought back the retort that came so easily to his lips. *Was that all? What more could there be?* A man would have to be blind not to notice the gaping spaces on the town house walls where fine oils had hung, or deaf not to hear the echoing of footsteps on hardwood floors where expensive, woven Axminster rugs made in the tradition of Thomas Whittey had muffled footsteps right up until this morning. And

1

that was just the beginning. The loyal housekeeper's artful arranging of furniture could no longer obscure the fact that the rooms—even the public rooms—were empty of many familiar pieces. The more discerning eye would have noticed long ago that the cabriole-legged tables next to the sofas were devoid of porcelain knickknacks, brass elephants, and other sundry items brought from the family's shipping interests in India—interests that had not kept pace with the needs of the estate.

"Yes, Mr. Lawbee. That is all." Gannon inclined his head graciously. "I thank you for Christie's discretion in this matter. My solicitor will contact you and handle the paperwork." Gannon tried to look nonchalant, as if auctioning off intimate household items were an everyday occurrence for a member of the peerage. By God, he'd keep his pride until the last, even if he hadn't a penny with which to support it. His father had always said there was more to being a gentleman than deep pockets. However, deep pockets definitely helped.

Gannon rang for Benton, the butler, to show Mr. Lawbee to the door, determined to stick to protocol for appearances' sake. He didn't think Mr. Lawbee was the type to gossip, but it would do no good for word to get out that Camberly had sunk so low as to show his guests to the door himself.

Certain that he was alone and unobserved, Gannon slouched into one of the remaining chairs in the drawing room. The earldom was broke, and it was on his watch, although it was not his fault. Camberly had teetered on the precipice of financial ruin for over a generation. In spite of his efforts to revive the flagging coffers, the estate had capitulated to its long-inevitable fate.

Seventeen years of ongoing agricultural depression were finally showing signs of outlasting the pocketbooks of even the most frugal peers, and in his case, the most inventive as well. He'd seen trouble coming and had done his best to protect against it. He'd tried various investments—commercial shipping and even the Exchange. Nothing had paid off in large enough dividends to do more than forestall the inevitable.

Gannon needed an infusion of cash, but there was nothing outside of the entailed estates left to sell, nothing left to act as collateral that might entice a bank to advance him a sum significant enough to pull Camberly out of its slump.

It didn't matter. A loan wasn't the answer. Any loan he took out would have to be paid back, and that patently could not be done. At any rate, a loan would solve nothing beyond providing temporary succor for the ailing earldom.

At thirty-three, he was the patriarch. He had great-aunts in the country at the family seat, a seventeen-year-old brother away at school, and a thirteen-year-old sister on the brink of womanhood, all counting on him to find a way through this crisis. It was time for his backup plan.

"You're going to do what?" Sir Garrett Atherton, Gannon's best friend from their days at Eton together and now renowned legal counsel for the Crown, said in hushed tones of disbelief in the sanctity of White's two hours later.

Gannon chuckled at his friend's shock. "You heard me. I am going to America."

Garrett, who was always in control and so very cool, gave a gratifying sputter at having been taken by surprise. "My dear friend, I say this with kindness, but, considering your financial difficulties, I hardly think gallivanting across the ocean on holiday is a wise idea."

Undaunted by his friend's logic, Gannon pushed ahead. "I would hardly call my trip a 'holiday.' After all, I am heiress-hunting."

"This is patently the most outlandish scheme you've come up with. Ever," Garrett huffed. "I should come with you to keep you out of serious trouble."

"Oh, no, I need you here, Garrett," Gannon said carefully. This was the tricky part of the plan.

Garrett's dark gaze grew wary. "Why is that, Gannon? The last time I went along with one of your plans, I nearly ended up suspended for spying on the headmaster's daughter."

Gannon laughed at his friend's caution. "*Nearly.* That's all. There's a big difference between a *fait accompli* and *nearly.* I didn't let you get caught, did I?"

"Well, no," Atherton admitted. "Still, it was a near thing."

"All I need this time is for you to hold off the creditors for a few months. I'll be back in September with plenty of money. By fall, I won't have to worry about financial security again," Gannon said with more confidence than he felt. This was a big gamble—the last gamble, in fact. If he squandered this final chunk of money from Christie's on a bride-finding gambit in America and failed, it would all be over for good.

"A few months? Until September?" Garrett practically came out of his chair. "That is downright audacious. It gives new meaning to keeping the enemy at arm's length. I am a barrister, not a miracle worker. Do you know how desperate your situation is? I am not talking about debts to a Bond Street tailor or a carriage maker. I am talking about mortgages here."

Gannon gave a covert glance about the room to see if they'd drawn any stares. Garrett's voice was louder than he'd have preferred. "Of course I know the extent of my debts," he hissed in a lowered tone. "What would you have me do? Sit back and wait for the creditors to come for my estate? For my home?"

Garrett spread well-manicured hands on his knees in a gesture of acceptance. "You know I don't want that. I will do what I can." He drew a deep breath and drank from the crystal tumbler at his elbow. "Still, what you propose is nothing short of craziness."

Gannon tossed off the rest of his own glass. "It's not as crazy as one might think. In fact, I'd say it's the future for us land-bound nobles."

Garrett Atherton leaned forward. He lowered his voice in deadly earnest. "It's the principle of the whole scheme. I am dismayed, and I use the term mildly, that an Englishman would consider selling himself to the highest bidder like a common doxy on the wharves."

Gannon stiffened at the rebuke. At its meanest denominator, that was exactly what his scheme reduced to. But he tried to ignore that, cloaking it in convoluted logic. It didn't help to have his friend voice those sentiments so bluntly. "Well, why not, Garrett? Those Americans have got millions and no restrictions over primogeniture. It's not like here, where heiresses are rare gems. Here, if a rich girl's got brothers, she gets nothing. Over there, fathers are happy to will it all to their daughters. It's prime pickings."

"We're talking about picking a wife, not an apple," Garrett said, making no effort to hide his chagrin over Gannon's callous attitude.

"We're talking about saving Camberly," Gannon retorted pointedly. "I've the got the looks and the title. I just need the fortune to go with it. After all, they've been doing it to us for a decade now—coming over here and hunting our titles like prized stags. Why not reciprocate? An heiress solves all my problems. American heiresses are more than a lark, you know. They're the future. Even the Duke of Marlborough is thinking of it. He's out of options while his brother, Churchill, has the American Jerome fortune behind him now, and he's not even the duke."

"Has it gotten that bad?" Garrett was aghast. "I hadn't heard about it lately."

Gannon nodded solemnly. All of society had been aware over the last several years of the items auctioned off from Blenheim, Marlborough's estate—the library, some nonentailed lands, the family jewels, the artwork, and the famous enamels.

Gannon spoke in a near whisper. "I have it on good authority that if Marlborough doesn't cross the Atlantic this year, he'll go next spring." He reached for his glass of brandy, tossing back the remainder. "And really, why shouldn't he go? Why should Churchill have a financially secure future when Marlborough's estate sucks up money like water on dry earth? For that matter, why shouldn't I, a responsible man of agriculture, have the financial security I need to run my estate?" His tone dared Atherton to challenge his plan.

"I can see you have your heart set on this madcap scheme," Garrett conceded. "I know from experience that there's no reasoning with you when you're like this. However, I have to try. I feel obliged to point out that having a plan and enacting a plan are quite different issues. How do you propose to take America by storm? More important, how do you think you'll meet the heiresses without being obvious?"

"Do you remember my friend Lionel Carrington?"

"The American?"

"Yes, the *wealthy* American," Gannon amended meaningfully. "He and his wife are sailing back to Newport, Rhode Island, for the summer in two weeks. Apparently, Americans flock to Newport from all reaches of the world at summer. Paris, London, Italy—the whole civilized world empties of them so they can have their Newport Season. Anyway, the Carringtons would love nothing better than to have me accompany them to Newport."

"Then it's already done." Garrett's tone was rueful. He nodded to the approaching footman. "It appears our luncheon awaits us. We shall share a last supper of sorts together and celebrate your departure."

The elegance of White's seemed more pronounced to Gannon's senses as they sat down to eat. Today, he was acutely aware of the pristine, starched whiteness of the tablecloths, the exquisite thinness of the crystal goblets, the perfection of the meal arranged artfully on china plates.

Even the conversation pricked his hypersensitive nerves. Across the table, Garrett tried to defuse his disapproval over the plan with easy chatter about horses—their shared passion—about the upcoming Ascot, and the summer regatta at Cowes. Expensive pursuits, to be sure.

Halfway through the conversation, Gannon realized with acute clarity that if he failed to secure financing for Camberly, he stood to lose more than an estate. He stood to lose a way of life—the way of life he'd been born to, the only way of life he knew. He would lose it not only for himself but for his sister and brother too.

Atherton leaned back after polishing off his filet mignon, wiped his mouth with a well-starched napkin, and looked Gannon squarely in the eye. "You're sure this is the only way?"

He didn't have to say anything more. Gannon knew to what his friend referred. But his decision was made. "It's either stay in England with no hope once this last batch of items is auctioned, or take Lionel Carrington up on his invitation. Only the latter offers any hope for a future beyond the fall harvest."

Garrett nodded his acceptance. A wry smile made a modest appearance on his lips. "If you are set on this course, then this calls for a toast." Garrett motioned to a nearby waiter. "A bottle of Champagne over here. Camberly and I are going to celebrate!"

Surprisingly, Gannon did feel like celebrating. The decision was made. This was a real chance to do something positive—and permanently—for Camberly. For the first time in months, he felt as if he were taking action, and it felt good.

Garrett poured the chilled Champagne and offered an oblique toast in a voice easy to be heard if one strained his ears. Gannon noticed that many did. The burst of excitement at their table had drawn the quiet attentions of their fellow diners. It would be all over town that Camberly and Atherton had been in high spirits over lunch.

Gannon clinked glasses with Garrett. "You're quite the showman, arranging for us to be seen in good humor on the very day my household goods are sent to auction. What will people think?"

Garrett chuckled. "They will think they've lost their

bets. I am tired of the town speculating on the exact date of your ruin, my friend."

Gannon laughed loudly, drawing more stares in their direction. He'd seen the betting book downstairs. It was full of wagers about his financial future.

Garrett raised his glass again and said ambiguously, so that eavesdroppers could draw whatever conclusions they wanted, "Here's to a change in your fortune."

"Here's to good sailing. Here's to a Newport summer," Gannon replied, lifting his glass to drink, ignoring the prick of conscience that rebelled at the cold thought of trading his title for cash, of picking a wife for her fortune, at putting aside any and all emotion. Emotion wouldn't keep him warm if Camberly went on the block.

Two weeks later, Gannon stood next to the exquisitely dressed Lionel Carrington and his lovely wife, Stella, at the rail of the *Bothnia,* Cunard's elegantly appointed transatlantic steamer, as it slipped its moorings in Liverpool to the cheers of passengers and the well-wishers on the docks. He waved to his brother Andrew, his sister Moira, and his Great-Aunt Lily who insisted on seeing him off. He thought of one more detail to tell Andrew about the summer wheat. He cupped his hands and yelled amid the shouts around him.

Lionel Carrington elbowed him in the ribs. "I am sure that whatever you have to say, you've already said to the lad a hundred times. Relax, Gannon. You'll be home for the harvest."

Gannon laughed at himself and sighed. "I am sure you're right. It's just that he's only seventeen, and the whole responsibility for the estate lies with him while I am gone."

"And with your very capable steward," Lionel reminded him. "Andrew shows a lot of promise. Your brother is growing up. He's not the same gangly lad I met two years ago." Good-naturedly, Lionel winked. "You have to face it. He'll be courting girls and dancing at the assemblies soon. Then he'll be begging you to take him up to London."

Gannon gripped the railing and assented. He'd noticed Andrew's maturity during his quick visit to Camberly over the past two weeks. It had all been a whirlwind. Once he'd decided to join the Carringtons, he'd spent four days concluding business in London, settling accounts with Christie's so that the sum of the sales would be placed in his personal account at the Bank of London. He arranged for the Camberly town house to be leased by foreigners looking for prime property to rent during the Season just getting under way. The rent and the enormous deposit he had required of them would see his aunts and siblings through the summer in the country.

With family and finances taken care of, Gannon had paid a visit to his tailor to order the requisite wardrobe for Newport. It went against his principles to spend money so lavishly on a wardrobe at such a time, but if he was to cut a compelling swath through Newport society, he had to go looking the part.

His remaining time had been spent on a mad dash to Camberly, balancing the ledgers and going over everything with Andrew, who had solemnly accepted the duties of Camberly without a flinch. His brother had understood with a maturity beyond his years that this trip to America was not a selfish pleasure fling. Moira had smiled dreamily at the prospect of impending romance. Gannon hadn't the audacity to crush her girlish notion that he was off to rescue a princess and bring her home to Camberly to live happily ever after.

Gannon stayed at the railing until the dock faded from view and the open sea lay ahead of them. They had sailed with the late-afternoon tide. Now the spring sun started to lower in the sky, giving way to twilight and stars twinkling like precious gems nestled in dark velvet. The faint clink of glasses and soft piano music came from the grand salon, reminding Gannon that his first night at sea was about to begin. In many ways, it was more than a first night at sea; it was the first night of a new life.

Chapter Two

W as this all there was to life? Audrey St. Clair made a complicated move with her ivory fan of Battenberg lace to hide a yawn from the sea of suitors vying for position around her chaise under the shady elm.

To her credit, she recognized that the day was exquisite in all ways, from the pleasantly warm June weather to the thrill of cold Champagne served in the afternoon. The annual Casino picnic was spread out before her, an elegantly appointed affair with its white canopies dotting the lawn that looked out over the blue Atlantic, and excellent lobster patties on silver trays served by footmen.

Yet she was bored—she who should have reveled in being the belle of the day in her expensive Worth gown of fine white India cotton and besieged by the attentions of Newport's finest young bucks, each one of them with a fortune at his disposal to rival her daddy's own. However, none of the young scions or their fortunes moved her to do anything more than make polite conversation.

Her gaze wandered from the group immediately around her to rove over the others present. They were the same collection of people who had been at the Randolph ball the night before, the same people she saw every day taking the air up and down the length of Bellevue Avenue. They were all the same—many of whom she saw socially in New York throughout the year. There wasn't a stranger among them. Did any one else notice? What was wrong with her that she could not pretend this picnic was somehow different from countless other similar events plotted on the summer calendar? Did no one else want to scream at the monotony of it all?

Suddenly she felt the overwhelming need to escape. She rose from her chaise and snapped her fan shut. "Excuse me, gentlemen." She gave a smile but no explanation for her absence and wound her way through the throng of well-meaning suitors until she'd won free of the crowd. At last she was blessedly alone on the tip of the bluff, staring out over the ocean, watching the waves roll into shore, the powerful pulse of the surf reaching her ears even at the cliff's height. In the distance, a yacht rounded the corner of a bluff farther east and headed toward her. If she had access to such a vessel, she'd sail in the opposite direction, away from all the pretensions and social-climbing nonsense of her world. The yacht passed the bluff she stood on and pulled up to the little dock located beneath the picnic area.

For a moment, Audrey felt a spurt of excitement. Maybe the boat carried new people, people she didn't know. Three people exited the yacht and took the steep wooden stairs leading up to the picnic grounds. Audrey wished she had a telescope to better view them. From her vantage point, she couldn't see them very well once they mounted the steps.

It probably didn't matter. She most likely already knew them. How could it be otherwise? Strangers were not welcome in Newport. She could always go back to the picnic and find out. She cast a glance at the set of stairs near her on the bluff; they led down to the sandy strip of beach. Or, she could go down to the beach, take off her shoes, and carefully wade in the surf. She opted for the latter.

Gannon Maddox shook hands graciously and kept a polite smile on his face throughout the innumerable introductions while Lionel and Stella toured him about the picnic. By four o'clock, he had to fight the urge to cringe when Lionel said for the hundredth time, "May I introduce you to the Earl of Camberly? He is summering with us over at Rose Bluff." Gannon felt he might as well have worn a halter and shown everyone his teeth. Goodness knew, he was decked out in his best "tack and harness"—a white summer suit of cool, spotless linen, and a hat to ward off the sun.

The news of his arrival had circulated throughout the

picnic like a ripple on a pond. Fathers smiled broadly and pumped his hand in the gregarious American custom. Mothers quietly urged fathers to introduce the family, and there had been a stream of conversations beginning with the phrase, "May I present my daughter . . ." Apparently no reference check was necessary if one carried the requisite title.

The girls curtsied and giggled, some of them barely out of the schoolroom by English standards. All of them butchered the appropriate address. He'd been "your highness"-ed and "your earlness"-ed all afternoon. But through it all, he'd not blanched. He'd made conversation, overlooking their silly errors, and complimented them on their hats or charm.

During a quiet moment, Stella pressed a glass of chilled Champagne into his hand. "You're doing splendidly, Camberly. They're not like our girls back home, are they?" She smiled fondly at a passing group of young debutantes headed for the shade of a nearby tree. They were giggling and failing miserably in their attempts to look discreet as they walked by the earl. "But they're good girls, just high-spirited. That's how it is over here. You'll get used to it." She gave him a supportive pat on the arm.

Gannon inclined his head. "I appreciate your commiseration, Stella." Lionel's wife was English, and in the past three weeks since their departure from London, he'd come to rely on her as a connection with home. It helped beat the homesickness he'd been surprised to feel. He'd never been away from Camberly or England with the exception of his Grand Tour after Oxford. Even that had been cut short with his father's sudden death. Afterward, Camberly had been his life. There'd been no time for trips abroad. And lately, there'd not been the blunt for them either.

"It will get better once you stop thinking of America as a copy of England. For all their Anglophilic passion, this is a place all its own." Stella laughed softly at his side.

"What do you think of it all, Gannon?" Lionel approached, stooping slightly to kiss Stella on the cheek. Unlike Stella, who insisted on addressing Gannon by his title, Lionel was American to the bone and had no such compunction.

"We were just making comparisons," Gannon said obliquely.

"Well, here we are. A toast to our safe arrival." Lionel raised his eyebrows meaningfully, and the threesome clinked glasses.

Gannon knew Lionel meant more than just the uneventful crossing on the *Bothnia.* He'd been introduced, his title and association with the well-loved Carringtons having sealed his acceptance into the tight Newport circles. "If our business is done for the day, Lionel, I think I will leave you two to catch up with old friends, and I shall wander about on my own."

"If you're sure?" Lionel prevaricated. "I don't want you to be a wallflower."

Gannon laughed. "Hardly that. When have I ever been a wallflower? I'll be fine."

He set off, Champagne in hand, to see the picnic grounds. His first thought was that Moira would love seeing it. The canopies, the beautiful plates of food laid out like artwork, the fountain centerpiece on the buffet table spouting Champagne, the women in their summer dresses and beribboned hats. He would have to write her an extremely good description of the event, leaving out, of course, the more sordid undertones—that amid all the splendor of the afternoon, he'd felt lower than a common doxy. If he did, it was his own fault. He could imagine what Garrett would have to say to that. This was a bumblebroth of his own making. He'd put himself up for sale; he could expect to feel no less.

Gannon reached the edge of the bluff and leaned on the railing overlooking the ocean. The view was quite spectacular. Blue went on as far as he could see, and beyond that was England, two weeks away. He thought of Camberly, and it gave him strength. There was no shame in doing what was necessary.

A speck of white caught his attention farther down the beach, stark against the navy hue of the waves. Someone—a female someone, it looked like—was enjoying a walk in the surf. Inexplicably intrigued, Gannon followed the path to the stairs and went down to the beach.

He would never be quite sure what compelled him to set down his Champagne glass and behave so recklessly as to leave the party and wander off on his own. Goodness knew, it was bad form to simply leave, especially when one was fast becoming the most interesting curiosity on display. Then again, perhaps that was precisely why Gannon found himself on the beach, shucking off his shoes and rolling up his linen trousers before he could second-guess himself.

He was starting to appreciate the adage, "There is safety in numbers." Among the ton, he hardly stood out as a rarity. Here, he was a rarefied specimen. The economics of supply and demand could not be illustrated in starker relief.

Gannon bent down to scoop up a handful of pebbles. He tossed one across the waves with a flick of his wrist, gratified to see the little rock skip three times. He threw another, trying hard not to think of the stream on Camberly's western border where he had lazed away the long summer afternoons of his youth, skipping pebbles with Garrett.

"Is three skips the best you can do?" A feminine voice took him unaware as he studied the remaining pebbles in his hand, searching for a likely candidate.

Gannon looked up from his survey, unwilling to be embarrassed over being caught at his simple pleasure. "Do you think you can do better?" He fronted a charming smile, recognizing the girl in white before him as the one he'd seen from the bluffs earlier.

Up close, she was stunningly beautiful. London society would have labeled her an "original" instantly simply

for possessing flawless cream skin, hair the color of
smooth milk chocolate, and eyes reflecting the English
preference for blue the shade of robins' eggs.

Those striking blue eyes of hers danced at the prospect
of a challenge, her rose lips tilting up in a smile. "Yes, I
think I can do better." She gave an entrancing laugh and
peered into Gannon's open palm, poking around the remaining pebbles, unaffected by the reality that she was
touching bare male skin.

It did not escape Gannon's notice that no self-
respecting London debutante would have been caught
in such an indelicate position or without her gloves on.
But Lionel and Stella had warned him plenty of times
that American girls did not follow London's dictates
when it came to decorum. Everything he'd seen today,
this lovely beauty included, proved the Carringtons to
be quite right.

"Aha!" The girl held a pebble aloft in triumph. "Perfect. It's smooth and round," she declared, giving Gannon an impish grin. "Now, stand back and watch."

She flicked the small stone expertly out over the waves
and crowed with unabashed delight when it skipped four
times. "There, that's how it's done. It's all in the wrist,"
she exclaimed in high spirits.

"Perhaps it's all in the pebble," Gannon countered
teasingly. "It could be that that pebble would have gone
just as far for me." He pretended to scrutinize the remaining stones in his hand. "I don't think there's an-

other one its equal in this bunch. Alas." Gannon dropped the stones onto the beach and dusted off his hands.

"You're English?" she asked suddenly.

Gannon gave a nonchalant shrug, trying to make light of it. He'd been having fun for a moment, not being anything. "The accent is a dead giveaway, is it not?"

The girl laughed again. "I didn't notice it at first."

"Well, that's understandable. I hear stone skipping can be quite thought-consuming," Gannon parried. "But I am English, and, from the sounds of it, you're not," he said, returning to the topic of conversation.

The girl cocked her head to look up at him, shielding her eyes with a hand against the glare of the sun. "You're quite funny. I had been led to believe Englishmen weren't all that droll on the whole."

Gannon put a hand to his heart. "I am fair wounded! I assure you that Englishmen are indeed possessed of some modicum of wit." He gave her a teasing glance, then studied her in mock consideration. "It makes me wonder what else you've been misinformed about in regard to England."

"My girlfriends who've been abroad tell me that the standard English gentleman is a sallow fellow given to slenderness and a slouch." She answered frankly. "But I can already see that they are much mistaken in that assumption."

It was Gannon's turn to laugh heartily. He drew himself up, purposefully exaggerating his already excellent posture. "Is that so? I suppose the American male is a preferred specimen, then? Amazing, we were able to defeat Napoleon years ago with all the characteristics you've imbued us with."

"Pax!" she cried just as a large breaker roared toward shore, crashing worrisomely close to their bare feet.

In a swift movement, Gannon had his hands at her waist, sweeping her out of harm's way, avoiding most of the wave's residual foam. His own feet and ankles weren't so lucky. Gannon stifled a yelp at the cold Atlantic soaking. "Is it always this cold?"

"Yes, we consider it quite bracing," the girl laughed. "Are you all right? Your clothes aren't wet, are they?"

"I'll manage." Gannon shook out his damp impromptu cuffs, silently hoping the salt water wouldn't damage the fabric permanently.

"There's a boulder a short way down the beach that's in the sun. Come on, I'll show you, and you can dry out a bit," she offered, holding up her skirts in one hand and making her way barefoot over the pebbly beach, much to Gannon's astonishment.

She looked back over her shoulder. "Since we are to be sharing the beach, we should probably introduce ourselves. I'm Audrey."

Gannon smiled, taken in by her easy manner. "I'm Gannon." He could not recall the last time he'd introduced himself by his given name. Everyone had called him Camberly for ages, even his great-aunts. A select few called him Maddox. But aside from Moira and Andrew and Garrett, no one called him Gannon, likely because *Gannon* meant nothing to anyone, and *Camberly* meant everything. He'd long ago come to the realization that his sole importance to society was that he was the living embodiment of a title, of a place. His own consequence was of little merit outside of that.

They reached the rock and clambered onto its broad back, Audrey making the scramble without any of his offered assistance. The rock was warm, and he could still see the wooden stairs leading to the cliff in the distance. They hadn't come too far, but far enough to evade prying eyes.

"So, what brings you here?" Audrey asked as they sat side by side on the big rock, enjoying the sun.

"I was invited by some friends," Gannon replied vaguely. The day was suddenly too pleasant to spoil with his realities. He wasn't ready to confess that he was an earl. Audrey was probably the only person in Newport who didn't know he was the Earl of Camberly.

His answer seemed to please her. "That's good. So many Englishmen come here to hunt heiresses."

Gannon was immensely glad he'd avoided mentioning that. Still, he had to marvel at the slight bitterness in her tone. "Jealous, are you?"

"Heavens, no!" Audrey exclaimed. "There are plenty of girls who want Englishmen's titles, and they're welcome to them. It's not a life for me, though. I don't want to be tucked away in a drafty house in the country, pouring my efforts into a pile of crumbling stones and an impractical lifestyle." She tossed him a sidelong glance. "Does that offend you?"

There it was again, that American bluntness. Gannon tossed an errant pebble into the waves. "What part would I find offensive? The part where you deride dear Britannia, or the part where you speak your own mind?" He held his stoic pose long enough for her to really worry. Then he grinned. "I've been warned about you American girls. And forewarned is forearmed. I was prepared for such an outburst."

Audrey laughed up at him. "You're very clever for an Englishman."

"I like to think so."

"Modest too."

They sat in affable silence after that, appreciating the late afternoon and the cooling breeze that came up off the waves. It was deuced odd to enjoy a woman's company so easily, Gannon thought, covertly studying his companion. He barely knew her name, knew hardly anything about her that he could put down on paper, yet he felt he *knew* this Audrey.

Too bad she wasn't an heiress. Too bad she was so poorly disposed toward Englishmen. It would be nice to be married to someone with whom one could trade easy banter, sit with and not have to talk, someone who would be pleased to share a quiet afternoon of stone skipping. When he had concocted this scheme, he'd not taken time to think of what he'd be sacrificing by putting himself at the mercy of the highest bidder. This afternoon, he'd had a chance to see firsthand what he'd be giving up.

"The tide's coming in," Audrey said at last, nimbly sliding down from the boulder. "I should head back before my parents discover I haven't simply slipped home ahead of them."

She was so nonchalant that Gannon had the impression the intrepid girl might have done this before—this heading down to the beach unchaperoned—on several occasions.

Audrey shook out her skirts to minimize any undue wrinkles in the white cotton. She flashed Gannon a brilliant smile that lit up her face. "Perhaps I will see you around. Newport's not so large, really."

Gannon inclined his head. "Perhaps we'll meet again," he affirmed, but inwardly he doubted the words. As she moved down the beach, he thought that unless she moved in the lofty circles of the Carringtons and the Astors, he would not encounter the intriguing miss with chocolate hair again.

And he was skeptical that she did move in such exalted groups. He rather questioned that parents of a lovely heiress would let her roam the beach at will without so much as a maid or governess in attendance, even if they were Americans. Of course, her gown had been fine. He had noted the excellent quality cotton and exquisite lace trim, but many middle- and upper-class people were beginning to spend money on nice clothes in

the hopes of aping their millionaire betters. In all likeli-
hood, Audrey was the daughter of a well-to-do merchant.
He wouldn't see her again.

It was for the best, Gannon thought, recognizing only
after she'd gone how compromising their situation
could potentially have been. Based on what the lovely
Audrey had shared, she wouldn't welcome finding out
he was an earl, nor would she welcome being leg-
shackled to him and his "drafty" country house. Yes, he
was certain she wouldn't relish the prospect any more
than he did, knowing that a moment's foolishness could
have cost him Camberly Hall forever. At least that's
what he told himself as he tried with only marginal success to push aside thoughts of Audrey and focus on the
task at hand.

Chapter Three

Audrey brought the Beethoven piece to a close with a resounding chord that sent the conservatory of her parents' grand summer "cottage" reverberating with the force of it. Her music instructor, a slender German fellow of indeterminate years named Heinrich Woerner, applauded enthusiastically from the edge of his Louis XV chair. But Audrey could feel her mother's abject disapproval without turning around.

She took a moment to bask in her instructor's appraisal. She deserved the praise, and she knew it. She had dedicated herself to the task of mastering the Beethoven piece for months. She needed a perfect Beethoven piece in her portfolio as part of the admission process to a highly acclaimed Viennese conservatory where she'd secretly applied for entrance.

Not even Heinrich Woerner knew what she had done. So precious was her secret, she couldn't risk telling a single soul. Mastering this final piece put her one step closer to her dream of studying and playing piano professionally. Now all she had to do was wait for the acceptance letter and survive the summer without becoming engaged.

The last was easier said than done. Evading her parents' matchmaking efforts was no easy task. Their persistence and social connections, combined with her father's obscene amount of wealth acquired in textiles, made her a very eligible candidate for marriage.

"Well done! Well done, Fraulein." Woerner stood up and walked toward the piano while her mother gave an audible sigh.

Her parents tolerated her passion for the piano, going so far as to bring Herr. Woerner out to Newport once a week in the summer for instruction. But Audrey knew they wouldn't have tolerated it if music had been unacceptable as an activity for a cultured, well-bred daughter. Still, there were limits to what they would tolerate. They would definitely not countenance their daughter's going off to Vienna alone and taking up a career of performing the piano publicly.

"Shall we try the new piece?" Woerner suggested eagerly. "I think we have just enough time."

"Oh, I don't think so." Audrey's mother, Violet St. Clair, swiftly rose, her tone polite but not warm. "The hour has passed so quickly. Audrey has to dress for the evening, and I wouldn't want you to miss your boat, Herr Woerner. It's five o'clock already."

It was common knowledge that the Fall River Line steamers that ferried passengers from Newport to New York left for their overnight trips in the evening. Audrey could imagine her mother's status-conscious horror over being burdened with the presence of a shabbily dressed music tutor in the house for the span of an extra day if he missed the steamer.

Woerner might admire Audrey's skill, but he knew which side his bread was buttered on, and he acquiesced with her mother's dismissal of him. "Then we'll start with the new variation first next week." He gathered up his battered traveling valise and headed toward the door.

"Speaking of next week, Herr Woerner," her mother called out. "Perhaps you could teach my daughter to play something more ladylike."

Audrey watched Woerner's shoulders sag at the "suggestion," which all three of them knew wasn't a suggestion at all. Violet St. Clair didn't make suggestions. She gave commands. There were some in Newport who said only Violet St. Clair dared (and had permission) to advise Caroline Astor with singular regularity.

"As you wish. I can suggest some *lieder* by Schubert that would be quite becoming for a young lady." Woerner gave Violet a stiff bow and exited quickly. Probably, Audrey thought uncharitably, before her mother could make another demand.

"Mother, you don't have to badger the poor fellow," Audrey said, turning on the piano bench to face her.

"Darling, why do you insist on such music? Beethoven puts one into such an irritable mood." Violet swept toward the polished beechwood grand piano with the same innate grace with which she swept across Caroline Astor's ballroom to join Mrs. Astor on the revered red sofa.

"Beethoven is perhaps the greatest piano composer of our century," Audrey began, knowing it was futile.

Violet shook her head. "I vow, I don't know what's come over you. It's more than Beethoven, darling. Whatever were you thinking to wander off during the Casino picnic? You were unchaperoned, to say the least, and worst of all, you missed your chance to meet the Earl of Camberly."

That got Audrey's attention. "An Englishman?"

"Not any Englishman, an earl. Weren't you listening?" her mother snapped. "All the other girls got to make his acquaintance. You should have been first in line."

Audrey rose from the piano bench and said with more nonchalance than she felt, "What do I care about an earl? He's undoubtedly scandal-plagued and land-poor like the rest of them." She should have been more careful with her words. But her thoughts were racing as she thought of Gannon. Images flashed through her mind: trouser cuffs rolled up and damp from the waves, dark hair ruffled by the breeze. It was difficult to merge those free, natural images with the idea that he might somehow be connected to the arrival of the earl.

What was he to the earl? A brother? A friend? The thought of seeing Gannon again was irrationally exciting as much as it was dangerous. She wanted to see him again, but she didn't need an earl to fend off all summer any more than she needed Gannon letting it slip that they'd met before in a highly inappropriate manner. All she wanted to do was escape to her room and mull over what she knew. But her mother would have her say first.

"Not care? That's nonsense. You should care immensely. You're the richest girl in Newport. You deserve an earl's attention. His attention is yours by right."

Audrey sighed. Arguing with her mother wasn't going to facilitate a quick exit. But placation would. "I am certain I'll have a chance to meet the earl soon, maybe even tonight." The Casino's weekly ball was that evening. They'd be attending after a light supper at home with some of the St. Clairs' closest friends.

"You're probably right, darling," Violet said, somewhat mollified, if not surprised, by her daughter's change of tack. "Wear something pretty."

After rejecting the tenth gown her maid paraded in front of her, Audrey began to despair of finding anything "pretty" in her wardrobe. It wasn't that her wardrobe was short on elegant, Worth-created evening gowns. Most Newport debutantes recognized the necessity for at least eighty gowns to get through the summer. Violet had insisted on that number and twenty more for her daughter.

No, it was not the paucity of choices that caused Audrey to despair. She was distracted. She was going to see the elusive Gannon again. She was certain of it. The thought brought a strange thrill with it and an element of peril on two fronts. She was in danger from the earl, whoever he was, and her mother's incessant matchmaking efforts, but she was also in danger from Gannon.

She didn't want him either purposely or inadvertently exposing her secret. Such a tidbit that she'd spent an afternoon with a stranger on the beach would be the worst sort of gossip to have put about Newport and the fastest way to find herself engaged, Vienna becoming nothing more than a fading dream. Her plan for the evening was simple in the extreme. She had to find Gannon first and ask him not to say anything about their prior acquaintance. If he was keeping company with the earl, it wouldn't be hard to find him.

Audrey finally settled on a taffeta gown the color of soft butter. Although the trend in gowns for married women was bright colors, unmarried young women were expected to wear pastels. The butter taffeta stood out to her as being not so pale as white and not so conformist as the popular pink preferred by so many other girls.

The gown was trimmed and ornamented in robin's egg blue to match her eyes and to avoid any tendency to blend into the background, not that there was any chance of that with a gown by Charles Worth. The great man himself had deigned to design her gowns, declaring her slim figure perfect without flaw for carrying off the cuirassed bodice and trained skirts.

In all, Audrey had to admit the effect was stunning,

from the patterned blue Murano glass beads dangling from her shoulders acting in lieu of sleeves to the pearl-embroidered petticoat beneath the taffeta, hidden from public view.

Audrey surveyed the effect in the long pier glass in her rooms and was pleased. She looked regal, commanding, yet the gown gave her an air of beauty that softened her belligerent edge just enough. She slipped her feet into kid slippers dyed to match, her arms into long gloves that ended at her elbow, and snatched up a gauzy wrap in the matching blue to drape about her shoulders for effect. She was ready to face the evening and whatever it might bring.

Bellevue Avenue was already crowded with dance-goers when the St. Clair barouche entered the fray and made its way toward the east end of the Casino, where the theatre-cum-ballroom was located. Violet St. Clair wouldn't have planned it any other way.

"If we left earlier, we could have avoided all this," Audrey groused as they moved forward at a snail's pace. "I could have walked there faster."

"Never say so!" Violet snapped in what Audrey could only wish was mock horror. But it wasn't. Newport was run by women, and those women were run by Violet St. Clair and her select few friends at the top of the social hierarchy. Only the constant maintenance of status would maintain status.

Audrey grimaced and said with a touch of obvious sarcasm, "Oh, yes, I forgot. We have to give the plebians their show." Much of the crowding was due to the middle-class citizens and vacationers at Newport gathered to watch the ultrarich make their way to the night's entertainment.

Violet narrowed her eyes and focused on her daughter. "Audrey, never forget that here, even more than in New York, society is on display constantly to those of the other classes as well as on parade among itself. What do you think would happen, darling, if I simply disappeared into the country for a few months? Do you think I would have my position when I returned?"

It was a rhetorical question. Audrey waited for the customary answer.

"No, of course not," Violet supplied. "If I were to disappear, someone else would attempt to take my place. Every day is a subtle battle, Audrey darling, one I wage gladly for the sake of seeing my beautiful daughter well-settled with a husband worthy of her." Violet turned to her husband seated across from her and Audrey, his back to the driver.

"Doesn't Audrey look wonderful tonight? I think Worth has done her an especial favor. She'll outshine all the other young ladies, and she needs to. Don't forget, we must have an introduction to the Earl of Camberly, even a dance, one of the first waltzes if possible. We want people to know Camberly favors us."

Her father exchanged a long-suffering look with Audrey that didn't go unnoticed. Violet leaned across the carriage and rapped him with her fan. "A titled son-in-law wouldn't hurt."

"I suppose the next thing you'll say is that 'everyone is doing it,'" Wilson St. Clair added wryly. "Husbands are not things to be collected like so much bric-a-brac. They are forever, and one only gets to choose once. I want my girl to be happily settled with more than a title to see her through life."

Violet bristled at Wilson's scolding. "I'm not talking about shackling her to a monster. I hear Camberly is handsome and young."

"And broke, I don't doubt," Wilson groused. "I wish these English boys would learn to make their own money instead of marrying for it. Where's their pride in being a self-made man?"

Violet groaned. "If they worked, they wouldn't be gentlemen. It's the last distinction left between a gentleman and a rich merchant. I've explained this to you before."

Audrey stifled a groan of her own. *Explained this before* was an understatement. *Harped on the subject* was more like it. This was oft-plowed ground. "We're here." Audrey drew their attention to the Casino with its clock tower front, the east side of the building ablaze with lights for the occasion. People dressed in elegant clothes filled the promenade as they strolled toward the lights and the evening's entertainment.

"Remember," Violet whispered to Audrey as they

were handed down from the carriage, "an earl is addressed as 'my lord.' "

Audrey barely heard the comment, so eager was she to get inside and locate Gannon. If Camberly was to be present, she was certain Gannon would be too. She had to find him.

Inside, the balcony overlooking the ballroom floor was already crowded with viewers who had paid a few dollars to come and see the wealthy at play. Below, the ivory interior trimmed in gold finishings was elegant in its simple decoration.

Tonight's ball was sponsored by the Rose Club, a group of wealthy horticulturalists who gathered for the summer at Newport. They had decorated the ballroom throughout with luscious arrangements of flowers, several of the copious bouquets featuring the expensive but popular American Beauty rose. At two dollars a stem and not as long lasting as their tea-rose counterparts, they were the trademark of wealthy opulence. Already the air was delightfully scented with the delicate aroma of the blooms.

Violet took it all in with a practiced eye, commenting on and complimenting the exquisite decorations. Audrey hardly noticed, her eyes rapidly scanning the crowd. But to no avail. By the time the dancing started, she still had not found Gannon, and her dance card was full of acceptable partners, approved by her mother's judicious eye.

By the fourth dance, Audrey was heartily sick of

having the same conversation. Everyone wanted to talk about the new earl in town.

Between dances, the girls of her set gushed about his good looks and fine manners. A few even claimed to have seen him that night, although Audrey had yet to catch a glimpse of him in the crowded ballroom. During dances, her partners mentioned what a fine billiards player, horseman, and sailor the earl was reported to be. He was polite to mothers and sisters—even the ugly ones—one partner remarked indiscreetly. The earl had succeeded in making himself welcome to both sexes.

To Audrey's skeptical mind, that meant only one thing. A man making such a great effort to travel so far and to be so ingratiating was looking for a wife. She suspected she knew just what type of wife the man was after—a wealthy one who had not yet heard of whatever scandal of infidelity or finance he'd left on the other side of the Atlantic.

By the supper dance, Audrey concluded that the Earl of Camberly, whoever he was, did not carry any credentials that recommended him to her.

Gannon Maddox looked up at the ballroom's sky-blue ceiling, exquisitely painted with golden stars. "I'm quite impressed. The place is lovely," he commented to Stella Carrington as they strolled the perimeter of the vast room.

"There's a ball sponsored here once a week in the summer. Other nights, the seats are all put back in for theatre performances," she told him. "The place can seat up to five hundred."

"Very impressive," Gannon said again. "Is everything in America so large? It seems to be a common theme. 'Cottages' the size of country estates, incomes the size of colonial bankrolls."

"I'm afraid so." Stella laughed softly. "In the cities, the latest rage are buildings called skyscrapers. Lionel tells me there are plans to build several of these structures in New York. So far, it's just all speculation but . . ." Her voice trailed off, implicitly suggesting the act was as good as done. She turned the conversation to a new topic. "How are you doing, Gannon? Have any of the American girls caught your eye?"

Gannon shrugged. One had, but he knew only a name, and it was a useless fantasy to think anything could come of his afternoon on the beach. He could treat it as no more than an isolated moment in time, destined to be nothing other than a sweet, fleeting memory.

"They take some getting used to, as you said," he said noncommittally. In the past two days since his arrival, Stella and Lionel had filled his social calendar with no less than one yachting luncheon, a private picnic at the Elms, a visit to their second-row cabana at Bailey's Beach, a formal, twenty-course dinner at the Oelriches', and tennis at the Casino court.

He could not remember a time when the London Season had felt so demanding. But perhaps if he'd been looking for a wife on the Marriage Mart, he might have felt differently about the pace. The activities had been designed for him to meet as many girls as possible. Indeed, they'd succeeded to the extent that Gannon was laboring under the impression there were few men in Newport at all.

Lionel had laughed, assuring him that more men came down during the weekend and returned to New York for business during the week.

"Who's the richest girl in the room tonight?" Gannon asked.

Stella sighed and patted her friend's arm with her long, gloved fingers. "Oh, Gannon, don't let it come to that. I am sure there's someone who's rich *and* likeable."

"Until then, I'll stick with the richest. It's what I came for," Gannon said stoically, although the words stuck in his throat. He'd danced a few times already and couldn't imagine spending his life with any of his partners, no matter what size their fathers' bank accounts might be.

"Well, if you must know, the richest girl is the St. Clair chit," Stella said, glancing around. "I know she's here, but I haven't seen her yet. She's beautiful. Her mother's a social giant, bosom beaus with Caroline Astor. Her father is a modern Midas. Everything he touches turns to gold. His choice of investments influences everything on Wall Street. I'll make sure you meet her."

Stella paused for a moment. "I'm surprised you haven't met her yet. She was at the Casino picnic.

"Ah, there they are." Stella waved to an attractive

middle-aged couple and approached. The woman held herself stiffly in the best of postures with an air of coolness about her that suggested she was no one's equal. The man appeared more affable.

"Violet, it's good to see you. We didn't have a chance to talk at the picnic. I want to introduce our houseguest to you. This is Gannon Maddox, the Earl of Camberly," Stella said.

All stiffness vanished from the woman. "*Enchanté,* my lord." She focused all her attention on Gannon. He felt uncomfortable at the intensity of her perusal. Any minute now, she was going to ask him to open his mouth so she could check his teeth.

"I wish my daughter was here, my lord. You must meet her," Violet St. Clair said, apparently deciding he'd passed muster. "She's dancing right now, but perhaps you'd like to come into supper with us? We'd love to hear about England. Oh, here she is." The woman gestured to someone behind him. "My lord, may I present my daughter, Audrey St. Clair? Audrey, this is the Earl of Camberly."

Gannon turned and found himself momentarily stymied, struggling to reconcile the young woman who stood before him. The perfectly coiffed vision in butter and blue was none other than the blunt-spoken girl from the beach. His barefoot Audrey was the richest girl in the room?

It would seem to be a dream come true except for the look of rage on her face. She stared at him through angry eyes, and Gannon knew what she must be thinking—that he'd misled her that afternoon, that he'd deliberately obscured his identity, and she wouldn't be far from wrong. He'd had a chance to divulge his purpose in Newport, and he hadn't. He'd had a chance to give her more than a first name, and he hadn't. But neither had she. She had never once mentioned a last name he could have given to Stella for vetting. Still, he was willing to overlook such omissions. Apparently, she was not. While he was pleasantly surprised by the turn of events, she was outright horrified.

"So, it's you, is it?" she said coldly. Then she hastily added, to cover the implication of having met him before, "You're the one everyone's been talking about."

Chapter Four

Unbelievable! It was worse than her conjectures. Gannon Maddox wasn't just associated with the earl, *he was the earl.* Audrey silently scolded herself while her mother made gushing small talk with the handsome earl to cover her daughter's cold response to the evening's premier guest.

She should have known better. How was it that she'd overlooked the obvious that day on the beach? His answers had been as vague as he'd been well dressed. She should have seen immediately that he'd deliberately been obfuscating the truth. Englishmen with indeterminate goals simply did not vacation in Newport, and this one had been *invited.* No one got into Newport without an entrée.

Even if he hadn't let fall his invitation, it should have

been enough to note the excellent cut of his clothes and his clipped accent, reminiscent of the upper-class aristos who'd so recently become interested in wealthy American brides.

The clues had all been there regardless of his attempts to downplay them. Audrey had simply chosen to ignore them. It was rather surprising, and none too pleasing, to discover how easy it had been to trade in her common sense over a handsome face. But seeing him tonight, dressed exquisitely in evening clothes that defined his physique to perfection, the lapse was entirely understandable.

He was by far the handsomest man in the room. His attractiveness came from more than his good looks. The raven-dark hair, the smoothness of his chiseled jaw and straight nose, the piercing green eyes the color of moss were all features she'd noted before.

She had not noted the regal tenor of his bearing, the breadth of his shoulders, the narrow waist, and the strong legs. People, both men and women, wanted to look at him, wanted to be in his circle. He was charismatic in the extreme. Everywhere he went, his mere bearing commanded attention. It was positively riveting to watch him converse with her mother, who was enrapt beyond all else over his description of his stables.

Apparently, it was too riveting. An embarrassed silence fell on their little group, and Audrey realized she'd been caught in the act of staring.

"Miss St. Clair, do I have something on my face?"

Gannon—no, not Gannon, *the earl*—inquired, one hand searching his cheek to flick off whatever had attached itself there.

"Ah, no, not at all. Your face is fine, quite fine," Audrey said, flustered for a moment. Her mother gave her a raised-eyebrow look of scolding incredulity that said she could not believe the dearth of manners Audrey was displaying.

The earl smiled and smoothly continued with the discussion of his prized hunter, a roan stallion by the name of Brutus.

Fortunately, it was time to go into the supper room, and Audrey was saved from the opportunity to commit any more gaffes. To her mother's everlasting delight, the earl turned to Audrey. "Would you do me the pleasure of joining me for supper?"

It was all the invitation Violet needed. Whether the earl intended the offer just to Audrey or if he'd expected the entire family to join them, she'd never know. The moment the invitation was issued, Violet St. Clair accepted with alacrity and her usual smoothness, so that it appeared the earl had meant to ask them all.

"I'll arrange for the table by the windows. You'll enjoy the view," Violet said, gracefully moving into action to make the necessary arrangements for a table of six as Lionel Carrington joined the group and shook hands with Audrey's father.

Audrey did not doubt they'd be the center of attention. Everyone would be curious to see who the earl was dining with. Gannon offered her his arm and smiled. It was on the tip of her tongue to apologize for her mother's maneuverings, as subtle as they were, but she was not at all sure he saw the need for an apology. Perhaps he expected such attentions. Perhaps he even liked them. After all, she didn't know that much about him. She hadn't even known he was an earl. And she certainly didn't know if she could trust him. So far, she'd been lucky. He hadn't made any reference to a prior acquaintance. She had to speak with him to ensure that it stayed that way.

She motioned to Gannon to let the others go ahead of them into the supper room and indicated they should step off to the side. Gannon acquiesced with a smile, no doubt guessing her obvious reason for wanting a moment alone. Audrey didn't care how obvious her intentions were. She'd never dealt well in subtleties. That was her mother's department.

"So we meet again, Miss Sinclair, although I'd much rather call you Audrey as I did on the beach," Gannon said easily, slouching against a richly carved pillar, a lazy grin on his face. He instantly looked more like the man from the beach than the earl he'd been moments ago. It was a very dangerous transformation. She didn't need to recall how amiable, personable, he could be.

"So we do, Gannon, or should I call you Camberly or milord?" Audrey queried sharply, trying to take the measure of this enigmatic man.

"Gannon is what I'd prefer, with you at least," he

said, holding her eyes with an even gaze that threatened to unnerve her. A hidden smile played at his firm mouth. How dare he find any of this funny!

"I need to ask you for a favor." Audrey paused here, disliking the idea of needing a concession from a man she knew so little about.

"Anything," Gannon said. "Rock-skipping lessons, perhaps?" he joked lightly.

Audrey shook her head. "What I ask for is a little enough thing, but it is not a joking matter, at least not to these people." She gave a vague wave to include the crowd going into supper.

Gannon sobered. "I am sorry. I did not mean to make light of it. Ask me for anything."

"I need to have your word that you will not mention our encounter on the beach." Audrey searched his face for signs of his comprehension, signs that suggested he knew how important his compliance was on this matter.

"You have my word, Audrey."

"Miss St. Clair," she corrected sharply.

At her sharp burst of propriety, he gave his smile full rein. "Miss St. Clair, then." He made a small nod of acquiescence. "Rest assured, I'll say nothing on the subject."

Audrey breathed a little sigh of relief. "Thank you." She turned to go into supper, but Gannon's hand stayed her, warm and strong on her arm.

"Wait, Miss Audrey St. Clair. Now you have to do something for me."

She should have known nothing was given freely, not even one's word. Audrey was immediately alert, conspicuously conscious of the earl. Her senses were aware of the clean scent of sandalwood soap, the starched linen of his evening clothes, and of much else. Beneath the finery of a gentleman, she was keenly aware of the raw, unbridled maleness of him.

She wondered what price the earl would extract for keeping their secret. A stolen kiss, perhaps? Audrey felt her pulse speed at the thought of the earl's firm mouth on hers. The image was oddly appealing, sending a warm thrill shooting to her belly.

Gannon laughed at the look on her face, thankfully misunderstanding the reason for it. "Don't worry. What I ask for is a little thing." He borrowed her words. "I want a waltz with you tonight."

Most of dinner was spent on the usual questions. Which part of England did he come from? What kind of home did he have? And that was where the conversation stayed for a very long time. Gannon Maddox was clearly devoted to his home and to the two younger siblings in his care. Audrey could see that her parents were impressed with his descriptions of his home and countryside. Her father was intrigued with the level of Gannon's knowledge on farming and agricultural advancements.

But where they saw an interesting Englishman, she saw red flags. If Gannon Maddox loved his estate so much, worried over his summer crops endlessly, and missed his family, why was he here instead of there?

Audrey thought the answer was fairly straightforward. He was heiress-hunting in spite of his lack of mentioning it on the beach. Her original anger flared again, and conspiracies began to form in her mind. Had he known who she was beforehand? Had he gone down to the beach on purpose to corner her? Had he hoped to compromise her? Did he still mean to, regardless of the promise he'd made her? Worse, did she mind as much as she should?

Common sense told her she should mind very much. Audrey knew her mother. If Gannon so much as mentioned their encounter to her parents, they'd be married before either one of them could blink, and while that might suit Gannon's purposes, it did not suit hers. If he needed a fortune, compromising her would be the shortest distance to the goal.

The thought brought on a renewed sense of panic, her thoughts coming full circle. How could she have been so foolish as to entertain his company that afternoon when she was so close to achieving her dream of Vienna? She could stand to lose it all.

The room pressed around her, hot and loud with a thousand conversations. The excellent lobster stuck in her throat. She rose hastily, thinking only that she had to get out of the room. "Please, excuse me. I need some air." She was clumsy in her efforts to extricate herself from the closely spaced tables and chairs. Her elegant

Worth train got in her way, and she stumbled. Tears burned her eyes.

"Please, let me assist you," a quiet voice said by her side, a strong hand cupping her elbow. It was Gannon, and at the moment, she had no choice but to rely on him to steer her through the room. "Just walk with me, a few more steps, now a few more," he coached close to her ear, his voice pleasantly comforting. Within moments he had them outside and found them a bench in the coolness of the night air.

"Are you all right, Audrey?" he asked, paying no attention to her earlier request to call her Miss St. Clair. He pressed a handkerchief into her hand. "You're shaking. Are you cold?"

His evening jacket was off before she could answer, neatly draped around her shoulders.

She breathed deeply. The garment smelled of him, the sandalwood she'd noted earlier. She took another breath, feeling the air start to calm her. "I'm sorry to be a bother. I just felt sick for a moment. I am better now, thank you."

There was some truth in that, but she couldn't bring herself to tell him he'd been the reason for her upset. She wouldn't feel entirely well until he went away for good. As long as he was here in Newport, she was in danger. Too bad. He was quite charming, and she'd have liked to spend time in his company if the situation was different.

"Please, it is not necessary that you stay. You may go back to your dinner," Audrey urged. If he was out here

too long, her mother would be quietly reserving Grace
Church for the fall.

Gannon peered at her in the darkness. "I find I am
not convinced that you're feeling better, and I fear I
may be the cause of your upset. Have I done something
to bother you?"

"Done something?" Audrey's frustration broke, finally able to be directed at someone, something. "You
didn't tell me who you were on the beach."

"I told you my name. I did not lie to you."

"You did not tell me you were an earl!" Audrey replied,
her voice low and strident in her accusation.

Gannon's voice remained unsatisfactorily even and
logical. "You did not tell me you were an heiress—'the
richest girl in the room,' according to my sources tonight. You can imagine my surprise."

"That's different," Audrey huffed, although for the life
of her she couldn't figure out why at the moment. "One
does not talk about money in polite conversation."

"What would you have had me do, Audrey? Introduce
myself as a titled Englishman after you'd espoused such
a distaste for them? I, for one, was having too good a
time to ruin it."

That brought her up short and effectively quelled her
brewing tirade. The truth was, she'd been having fun
too. She'd liked talking to the Englishman on the beach,
so much so that she'd been willing to overlook the obvious about his presence in Newport. It wasn't fair to
blame him entirely. "I think I liked it better when we

were just Gannon and Audrey," she sighed, "instead of
the heiress and the earl."

Gannon laughed in the darkness, a rich, mellow, comforting sound. "Perhaps we can work on that."

He was so unfailingly polite, so unswervingly sincere,
that Audrey found herself dissembling in a most unladylike fashion. "Oh, no, you don't know my mother. You
have to go back in right now for your own good. The
longer you're out here with me, the more my parents will
get their hopes up." She could hear the panic return to
her voice. One would think she was on a run for her life,
from the fear her voice emanated.

"Hopes about what?" Gannon asked.

"Don't be obtuse," Audrey scolded, hardly believing
the man could be so dense. "What do you think parents
get their hopes up for when their daughter goes outside
with a handsome earl?"

"Ah. We're speaking of matrimonial hopes, I take it?"
Gannon paused. "You don't want to marry me?" Light
teasing colored his words.

"I hardly know you." Audrey was in no mood for
banter in spite of Gannon's efforts to the contrary. She
couldn't let him through her defenses so easily, even
though she was tempted. For all her reservations, she
was undeniably drawn to the Englishman.

"But you said I was handsome," he pressed.

That got a laugh from her. "Well, everyone says so.
The girls have talked of nothing else tonight but your
divine good looks."

"So is it me you're opposed to, or just marriage in general?" Gannon asked once the laughter between them faded.

"You mustn't take it personally," Audrey supplied quickly, not wanting to hurt his feelings. He'd been quite nice, and he deserved better from her. "I simply don't wish to be married."

"Especially to an Englishman," Gannon filled in. "I recall your specific points on the subject. I have an excellent memory, along with my posture."

Audrey blushed in the darkness, remembering her harsh words about drafty houses, empty pockets, and slouching physiques. "You must pardon my bluntness on the subject. In no way did I mean to impugn your Camberly Hall or your visit."

Awkward silence sprang up. "You're not the one who needs pardoning," Gannon said after a while. "That day on the beach, you were honest, while I was not. You have confided a bit in me, and now I find that I must confide a bit in you. You were right a moment ago when you said I wasn't entirely truthful with you. I am here heiress-hunting. I mean to find a rich wife so that I can save Camberly and my family."

It was just as she'd thought. But hearing the words didn't make Audrey feel triumphant. There was no glory in being right. She hadn't wanted him to be an heiress-hunter any more than he apparently wanted to be one. Instead of wanting to recoil in disgust, Audrey felt the sorrow that was so evident in his voice.

Instinctively, she reached for his hand where it lay on his thigh. She squeezed it gently. "I am sorry to hear that. You must love Camberly very much."

"With all my being," he said simply.

She nodded. She knew what that felt like. She loved the piano the same way, as if the instrument itself was her heart, but that was not a secret she could tell yet.

"You don't want to marry an heiress?" she ventured.

Gannon shook his head. "Will you keep my secret if I tell you? I want to marry someone who recommends herself to me beyond her bank account. Money is only money, as necessary as it is."

Audrey crossed her arms and sat back against the bench, irrationally liking the earl more and more as their conversation progressed. "It seems we are not such dissimilar creatures, Gannon Maddox. Neither of us is in a hurry to marry, but both of us are being forced to it by circumstances not of our making."

Gannon leaned back to join her, turning his head to the side so she could see the mischief playing in his mossy eyes. "What do you propose we do about that?"

Audrey smiled back, feeling better than she had all night. "I'll let you know. I am working on a plan that will see you rich and unshackled at summer's end."

"And what about you?" Gannon asked. "What do you get for all your machinations?"

"The only thing I've ever really wanted." Audrey stood up and shook out her skirts, carefully looping the long train about her wrist. "Now, come inside and dance with me, so everyone knows all is well."

Once inside, Gannon led her to the dance floor and fitted his strong hand against her back, moving them into the waltz with ease. "Tell me, Audrey," he asked, turning them at the top of the ballroom, "what is the only thing you've ever really wanted?"

She laughed up at him. "Why, my freedom, of course."

Chapter Five

Gannon watched the ocean rolling, blue and endless, from the wide bank of windows of the well-appointed sitting room the Carringtons had given him to use as an office of sorts during his stay. A half smile played at his lips as he reread the simple note that had arrived for him that morning—all two sentences of it—written in her forthright manner.

Audrey St. Clair had a plan. She would discuss it with him at the polo match later that afternoon.

Her letter was the best piece of correspondence he'd received. A plan that salvaged Camberly without requiring his matrimonial sacrifice would be ideal. But patently unlikely. It was fantastical to think that a twenty-year-old woman would have the answers he'd spent years looking for. Furthermore, he had no business trusting someone he hardly knew with such an important situation. He preferred the word *important* to *dire,* which was, unfortunately, just as accurate.

The other letter he'd received was from Garrett, posted during the latter week Gannon was at sea. Creditors had been highly concerned about the earl's absence from the country. Garrett assured him he'd scotched those concerns before they could become dangerous rumors. Yet such news was a sharp reminder of his purpose in Newport. The lure of Miss Audrey St. Clair was not a distraction he could afford.

Still, even knowing better, he could not banish the images of the prior evening completely. She'd been a breathtaking vision in her pale yellow gown at the Casino ball. Everything about her appearance had been orchestrated to perfection, from the way the color of the gown complemented her complexion to the blue trim that matched her eyes in subtle precision. She had been artistry in motion, a living, moving canvas for Worth's renowned craftsmanship.

But she was more than a mere mannequin come to life. He'd seen both her panic and her passion last night, and both had intrigued him, filling his restless night with suppositions. What was in this for her? What did she need her freedom for? He'd instinctively felt that her laughter on the ballroom floor was masking something deeper. She needed this plan to succeed because she had another plan that depended on it, but what that was, Gannon had no idea.

Lionel poked his head around the doorframe of the sitting room. "There you are. I thought I might find you here." Lionel nodded at the letters. "Not bad news, I hope?"

"No." Gannon dismissed the missive from England with an easy wave of his hand. "Just news from home—all the usual." *Creditors, debts, a flagging bank account*—nothing at all that the Carringtons dealt with.

"Good. I am glad to hear it. Stella's waiting for us so we can be off for the Casino. There's tennis today."

Gannon rose and smiled good-naturedly. "And I thought the London Season was busy."

Lionel clapped him on the back. "It takes some getting used to. The ladies keep a highly regimented schedule: morning rides at nine, shopping at the Casino at ten, swimming at Bailey's Beach at eleven, and dancing until sunup." Lionel laughed. "Thank goodness it's only for six weeks a year. How did you like the St. Clair chit last night?"

"I liked her quite well," Gannon said as they strolled through the wide halls of Rose Bluff to the entry, where Stella had the low-sided phaeton waiting. He found himself reluctant to discuss Audrey in terms of an object to be appraised.

Lionel raised an eyebrow at his friend's meager description. "That's all? She's an excellent choice. You could do no better."

Gannon took offense at that. "No better? In terms of what? Looks? Money? Connections?"

Lionel stopped in his tracks and threw his hands up in surrender. "Whoa! I didn't mean to raise a sensitive subject. I thought you were here for a wealthy bride."

Gannon faced his friend squarely. "I am, but I don't have to like it, and I don't have to subject any likely prospects to the same lowering experience I am becoming all too familiar with. We are people, after all, and entirely more than the sum of our balance sheets." Where had his cold detachment gone? He sounded like Audrey espousing her dislike of titled Englishmen.

"I am sorry, Lionel, I have lost my temper," Gannon apologized swiftly. "It is proving to be much harder to complete my mission than I had anticipated."

Lionel looked blankly at him. "Surely it's not the lack of willing candidates."

"No, it's not that at all. It's me," Gannon confessed. There was Audrey, desperately in love with her freedom, and there was the nightly sight of the elegant and inanely happy Carringtons themselves serving as poignant reminders of what Gannon had elected to sacrifice.

Lionel pierced him with a shrewd stare. "Ah, I am beginning to see. Well, perhaps the lovely Miss St. Clair will be at the tennis match this morning."

Gannon shook his head. "I have it on good authority she'll be at the polo grounds this afternoon."

"Then maybe things aren't a complete loss after all," Lionel offered, gesturing that Gannon should go ahead of him into the phaeton.

Gannon said nothing, merely climbed into the carriage and sat opposite Stella, complimenting her on the cut of her ensemble in an attempt to dislodge Lionel from the topic and change the conversation.

The match was already into its third chukker when Gannon and the Carringtons arrived later in the afternoon. Various styles of open carriages lined the perimeter of the field, filled with women holding delicate parasols over their heads to ward off the summer sun while their escorts studied the game. Today's match was an intraclub game between the Reds and the Blues. An occasional Hurrah! broke out from the crowd as someone's preferred team scored a goal, but otherwise Gannon thought people were more absorbed in their own conversations than they were in the match.

During the three-minute intervals between chukkers, some daring souls alit from their carriages and mingled. Gannon took advantage of the interval to seek out the St. Clair phaeton. He found it almost immediately. It was the conveyance surrounded with young men vying for Audrey's attention. Apparently he wasn't the only one who found Audrey's brand of beauty attractive. But he was the only who had carte blanche with her mother.

Violet caught sight of him nearing the carriage and gestured toward him with her closed fan, much the way Gannon imagined Moses had raised his staff over the Red Sea. The effect was the same. "Good afternoon, Camberly. Are you enjoying our American polo?" she called out. The people gathered around the carriage parted to make way for the earl, a few of the younger men muttering under their breath.

Gannon approached and took Violet's gloved hand, bending over it gracefully. "I am enjoying the match very much," he replied. "This place is a delightful venue for it."

"Of course you'd like it," Audrey put in. "It's an old farm." There was a conspiratorial gleam to her eyes that Gannon took up at once. He bowed in her direction. "You remember our conversation from dinner. I am flattered. Perhaps I could persuade you to show me about the grounds—that is, unless the match is too riveting."

Audrey seized on the invitation, gathering her skirts about her and moving toward him. He was ready to help her down. "I'd love to. Mother, we'll be back shortly."

Gannon noticed she didn't wait for Violet's approval, but the woman was smiling with supreme contentedness. "We'll stay in sight, ma'am," Gannon added, recalling Audrey's warning from the prior night.

"This place is technically called Glen Farm," Audrey began as they strolled arm in arm. "It's an old manor farm that dates back to the 1600s. There's nearly seven hundred acres here."

"It's lovely," Gannon said, meaning it.

"Is it like Camberly?" She turned her head toward him, tilting it upward beneath her parasol.

"A little. Camberly is much larger. We have a home

farm, a village, a church, fields, even a mill." Gannon couldn't keep the edge of pride from his voice.

"Is it entirely self-sufficient?"

"Nearly so. At least it was," Gannon conceded as they neared a small pond, still within view of the polo field but out of earshot. "Now, tell me your plan."

Audrey found a large stone and sat down, taking care to spread her skirts. She made a fetching picture in her pale blue carriage dress and wide-brimmed hat, but it seemed to Gannon that she took an inordinately long time to begin.

"Before I start," Audrey said, "are you willing to do what it takes to see this plan succeed? There is a modicum of risk involved."

"I am willing. You know I am." Gannon smiled in reassurance.

Audrey drew a deep breath. "All right. The problem, as I see it, is that my parents want me married, preferably to you or someone like you, and neither you nor I wish to be married to each other or otherwise at this time. In addition, you need huge sums of money, true?"

Gannon nodded, although he was starting to think that if he had to marry, he'd pick Audrey. She was beautiful, witty, and plainspoken. He could fall in love with that. He suspected he already was. But mentioning it would be premature, and it would certainly hamper her plan, whatever that might be.

"The solution needs only be temporary. We have to

survive until the end of the Newport Season. For purposes of my plan, I have defined *survive* for me as escaping an engagement and for you as remaining unmarried but in possession of enough money to save Camberly. To this end, I propose the following solution. First, you court me intently and exclusively. Let my parents and everyone else assume there will be an offer at the end of August. This will assuage my parents' need to find me a suitor, protect me from any unwanted proposals, and ensure my freedom when we publicly break things off at summer's end."

"And my money?" Gannon asked, more for form's sake than anything else. He'd willingly squire this multifaceted girl around just for the pleasure of her company if he hadn't been faced with a disastrous situation of his own. Being with Audrey provided surprises at every turn.

"Tut-tut, my impatient one, I am not finished yet," she scolded him with a coy look. "In exchange for your exclusive attentions, I will see to it that you're provided with the opportunity to make investments of the safest and highest order. I will show you how to do business in America."

Gannon shook his head. She wasn't the only one who could drive a bargain. "I need numbers. What are we talking about here? I need twenty-five thousand additional pounds a year to keep the estate debt free." He rather thought the number would swamp her. He personally found the sum staggering.

Audrey cocked her head to one side, considering. "You'll need more than that. We'll want to have something left to invest for the future. You need more than one year's bankroll," she said thoughtfully. "I can make you a hundred thousand British pounds."

Gannon hardly dared to breathe. "Are you sure?"

Audrey smiled broadly. "Well, you're going to have to work for it. I am counting on your charm. I can only open the doors for you and coach you a bit. But I am a mere woman, and there are limits to what I can do."

Gannon laughed. "I don't believe that for a minute."

Audrey extended her hand in the American gesture. "Shake on it? Partners?"

"Partners," Gannon affirmed, taking her hand. After all, he'd already lost everything else. He would be no worse off if her gambit failed than he was now. And he had a backup plan. He could still marry—although the idea was becoming more and more unpalatable to him by the day, and it was all Audrey's fault.

Audrey shook Gannon's hand with a confidence she didn't necessarily feel on the inside. If things went awry, it would be all her fault. The plan made sense, but it was one thing drafting it on paper and another actually launching it. Her freedom and his fortune were at risk. If the plan backfired, she could find herself betrothed to this man and toted off to England.

She wondered if Gannon realized the risk she took in trusting him to act his part. And she was trusting him.

Maybe not with money and an estate, which were very real things to weigh in the balance of their scheme, but she was trusting him with something just as valuable. If he chose to trap her at the end of the summer and refuse to cry off as they'd agreed, she'd have no recourse. After a summer of courting, it would be impossible to persuade her mother to back down. Violet would force the courtship to its logical conclusion if Gannon didn't play the jilt. Oh, yes, she didn't have money involved, but her risk was just as real.

Still, she didn't relish failing Gannon. The money he had available to stake on their venture was not replaceable. If she made a misstep, his funds would disappear and not be replenished.

"So, we're partners," Gannon said, releasing her hand after a brief squeeze. "What next?"

Audrey drew a deep breath. This was it. The game started now, the great gamble for her future. "Tonight. My family has been invited to Caroline Astor's for dinner and a night of cards."

Gannon raised his dark eyebrows at the mention of the great hostess herself. "Astor's? So soon?"

Audrey shrugged negligantly. "It's a small gathering, very informal." She gave him a wink. "Mrs. Astor won't serve more than eleven courses tonight."

Gannon laughed. "Only eleven? Heavens, I'd better eat a huge lunch, or I'll starve to death."

Audrey tossed him a saucy look. "Enough! I've heard

about your English Seasons. It's not as if the peers are all that frugal when it comes to setting the table. Tonight is just for close friends. It will be a select group and just the right sort of people for you to connect with in a situation where you can sit and talk."

Gannon gave her a piercing perusal that made her uneasy. She hoped he didn't sense her nervousness. "You're sure you know what you're doing?" Gannon said.

She smiled. "Absolutely. I learned business at my father's knee. We weren't always rich, you know."

They turned and headed back to the carriages and the polo field. "Really?" Gannon looked sincerely interested.

"Really," she affirmed. "I remember growing up north of Manhattan—out in the country, in a small but respectable brick house—until I was twelve. My father ran the local dry goods store. We were always comfortable, but one day, when I was eight, a textile mill opened not far from us, and father invested in it. Within a few years, he owned the mill, he bought another, developed connections to sell fabric, and things took off from there."

"That's incredible," Gannon said, a thoughtful look on his face.

"That's how it happens for many of the men who are here now." Audrey waved a gloved hand toward one of the carriages they neared. Her voice dropped as she gave Gannon a biographical survey. "That woman's husband made his fortune in wholesale grocery. They're worth three million dollars now after a lifetime of porting vegetables from country to city." She nodded in greeting to a woman who waved from another vehicle. "They made their money in dairy products."

"Cows?" Gannon asked, incredulous.

He didn't cover his surprise fast enough. "You're shocked," Audrey said. "Is it my talk of money that has you agape or the cows?"

"Both, I suppose," Gannon admitted honestly. The American millionaire and the methods of how he acquired his fortune were quite foreign commodities in his world of the peerage. "It's not as if I don't work," he offered up defensively. "It's just that I never thought of making money from it."

"Things are different in America," Audrey said mysteriously.

"Yes, I can see that they are." Gannon gave her a look that unexpectedly warmed her and left her with the feeling that he wasn't talking exclusively about business anymore.

They'd reached the St. Clair's phaeton, and Gannon handed her up under Violet's scrutiny.

"Will you be joining us tonight at the Astors'?" Violet asked as Gannon saw Audrey settled.

"It will be my pleasure. I appreciate the invitation's being extended. I hope that it won't be an imposition," Gannon said with the right degree of humility.

Violet smiled with delight, fixing Audrey with a pleased gaze. "Caro welcomes all my friends," she returned.

Audrey cast a quick glance at Gannon. She hoped he read all the messages contained in that simple sentence. From the short bow he made over her mother's hand, she was sure he had. Tonight would be important. For them both. There was money to be made and rumors to be hatched.

Chapter Six

Audrey dressed carefully for the evening in a peach gown of summer silk trimmed in tiny seed pearls to complement the simple pearl necklace that lay against her collarbone. The ensemble was ideal for an elegant but supposedly "informal" gathering at Beechwood.

During the short drive down Bellevue Avenue to Caroline Astor's Italian-styled villa, Audrey mentally ran through her game plan. She'd been dining at Beechwood since she was old enough to put her hair up. Tonight's dinner would follow the same pattern these evenings always followed. Guests would arrive a half hour before dinner and gather in the drawing room. Dinner would be a three-hour affair that allowed Caroline to parade her chef's excellence and her bank account's depth in front of her guests on the most expensive china in her extensive collection. Afterward, card tables would be set up, and everyone would engage in games of whist while exchanging the latest gossip.

Normally, the affair would bore her. Audrey could guess everything that would occur, right down to the conversations people would hold and whom they would talk about. But tonight, having the key to that knowledge was an advantage she wouldn't hesitate to use. Tonight, she was looking forward to dinner because Gannon would be there.

She hastily reworded her thoughts. The evening would be exciting not simply because Gannon was there but because of the challenge the evening posed on his behalf. She must keep their relationship in perspective and not lose sight of their mutual goals. Although they needed each other, that didn't necessarily make them bosom beaus. Gannon was still potentially dangerous to her. She'd do best to remember that she'd concocted this plan to keep her friends close and her enemies closer. Unfortunately for Gannon, he fit into both categories.

Gannon was already there when the St. Clairs arrived. It appeared he was just minutes ahead of them, greeting Caroline with his excellent manners and presenting her with a small, exquisitely wrapped box, which she accepted as her due before gesturing to Violet. "Violet darling, we must give Camberly a party—something English to remind him of home," she said. "Mr. McAllister can draw up the lists and the plans and consult the schedule for sometime in a couple of weeks. I think a picnic shouldn't be too hard to manage."

"A fabulous idea," Violet concurred, admirably hiding the elation Audrey knew must bubble beneath the surface of her cool demeanor.

"Audrey, be a dear and introduce Camberly around," Caroline suggested in her imperious tone.

Audrey didn't miss the calculation. Caroline and her mother had already decided the earl was to be hers. It sent a tremor of fear through her to know how quickly her fate had been decided and managed by the two of them. She wasn't the first girl to have her future so adroitly arranged, but she had a plan. It stiffened her resolve to know that only her plan stood between Vienna and a marriage in which her personal feelings were of no consideration.

"May I say that you look lovely this evening?" Gannon asked as she moved them across the opulent drawing room to a cluster of guests.

"You may. Remember, you must pretend to court me. Showing a little liking would not be amiss. What was in the present you gave Mrs. Astor?" she asked, her curiosity getting the better of her.

"Jealous, are you?"

"No. Merely curious."

Gannon leaned close to her ear. "It's a Limoges trifle box. Something practical to keep a diamond brooch in."

"Very good. You've done your homework," Audrey

complimented. Anyone who knew Caroline Astor knew she adored her diamonds; they were her signature jewel, just as black was her signature evening gown.

Audrey made the introductions and then stepped back from the conversation to let Gannon take over. By the time dinner was announced, Gannon had quickly won the confidence of the little group. Over the extensive dinner, Audrey watched silently as Gannon proved himself worthy of inclusion among the elite assembled.

"How do you find America?" Caroline Astor queried from her place at the head of the table, her husband absent as usual, spending his week in New York stoking the family fortunes.

"I find it a most excellent place," Gannon said to the table at large, since Mrs. Astor's question had silenced the rest of the conversations. "I am intrigued by all the business and industry, particularly the railroads. I think there is much to learn here."

"Hear, hear!" Wilson St. Clair applauded from his end of the table. "A man who appreciates vision is always welcome."

There was a chorus of "hear, hear" to follow Wilson's pronouncement. Audrey smiled at Gannon from across the table. The bait had been set. She would bet that after dinner, over port and cigars, Gannon would be introduced to his first business opportunities. The plan was in motion.

Gannon gave the St. Clair butler his card at precisely five minutes before five o'clock the next day. He'd been invited, ostensibly, to take tea with the St. Clairs. It would be the first time he'd have an opportunity to talk over the evening with Audrey.

If it had been up to him, he would have rushed over first thing in the morning, but he knew it simply wasn't *comme il faut.* One would no more call before one o'clock in Newport than he would in London. Unfortunately, Stella had him off at a yachting luncheon that afternoon, and he was unable to call earlier. Sensing his disappointment but attributing it to the fledgling stages of romance, Stella had smiled charmingly and said, "Keep her dangling, Camberly. Don't appear too eager."

"I have business with her father," he'd responded, but Stella was unconvinced. For that matter, he was too. It was true that he had business with Audrey's father, thanks to an intriguing discussion over port and cigars at Caroline Astor's. But that wasn't the reason for his impatience. He found he was filled with an inexplicable desire to celebrate with Audrey, to share with her all that had taken place after she and the other women had left the table.

To his credit, Gannon did try to explain his desire to see her again rationally to himself. Impending romance had nothing to do with it. They were co-conspirators after all. Of course he'd want to share with her how things were going. The urge to see her had nothing to do with simply wanting to share her company, to hear her opinions, or to be the recipient of that saucy smile she tossed his way whenever she teased him.

"This way, sir. The St. Clairs will receive you in the conservatory," the butler intoned, returning from wherever he'd gone with Gannon's card.

Gannon followed the fellow through the wide halls of Briar Cliff, the well appointed "cottage" the St. Clairs called home for eight weeks each summer, never guessing what a flurry of excitement his visit had conjured up in the room down the hall.

"Audrey, sit here at the window. The sun will catch your hair just so," Violet instructed in a hurried whisper. "Here, look like you've been reading." She shoved a slim volume of Longfellow's poetry into Audrey's hands. "I wish you had time to change. Your afternoon gown in celery green would be perfect in this setting."

"We're receiving a caller, not sitting for a portrait." Audrey grimaced and gave a sighing huff, plopping down on the window seat as instructed. She rather thought Gannon would laugh if he could see her mother's contrivances. "I doubt English girls go through so much nonsense." Audrey twitched at her skirt.

"Don't be ridiculous. Of course they do. Every girl has to make a good match. Even so, American girls have to try harder. We don't have titles to recommend us, only ourselves and our deportment. Sit up straight. Act like a countess. We want Camberly to see your potential." Violet sank onto the nearby settee in an artful pose, seeming to concentrate on the needlework in her lap.

The scene of domestic tranquility, Newport style,

made Audrey want to shudder. She *had* to get into the Viennese conservatory. How was she to escape all this otherwise? She did not want to become her mother, but what else was there for her here? How did the other girls stand it? Audrey knew she wasn't alone in her situation. Down the avenue at the Breakers, Alva Vanderbilt was overtly hanging out for the Duke of Marlborough in hopes of snatching him up for her daughter, Consuelo. The duke hadn't come over yet, but Alva was anticipating him. She'd been tracking the eligible duke's social and financial history for years, ready to run him to ground when the time came. Audrey was tired of the whole game.

The conservatory door opened, and the butler announced Gannon. *The Earl of Camberly.* She kept forgetting. It was telling that she couldn't bring herself to think of him as the earl, a titled English lord. It shouldn't have been that hard to do. He certainly looked every inch the artistocrat.

Today he was attired in a lightweight wool morning suit of charcoal gray that made his hair appear even darker than usual, and the subtle striping of his trousers made his legs look longer. Not that she should have been noticing such a masculine feature. Audrey promptly averted her gaze back to the text of her book.

Through her lashes, she saw her mother rise and greet the earl with amazing calm, considering what had transpired in this very room only moments earlier.

"Mrs. St. Clair, I am delighted to be received."

"Come and sit. We'll have tea shortly." Violet St. Clair gestured to a chair near the sofa where she'd been sitting. "Audrey, come and join us."

"Miss St. Clair."

Audrey felt his eyes on her as she set aside her book and crossed the room to join them. "How kind of you to call on us," Audrey said, coaching herself to remember the role their plan had assigned him as a potential suitor.

"I hope I haven't interrupted your reading?" Gannon nodded in the direction of the volume she'd left behind.

"Of course not." Audrey smoothed her skirts and sat down, feeling conspicuous and wondering if her mother noticed the stilted nature of the conversation. It was much more awkward than she'd anticipated, playing out two roles. She had to remember that her mother thought that she and the earl had only met twice now and both times in the company of large groups. With the exception of the stroll at the polo grounds, they had never been alone beyond their brief breather at the Casino ball to her mother's knowledge.

"Did you enjoy the supper party last night?" Audrey said quickly to cover up the silence.

Gannon relaxed into his chair, crossing a leg. "I did. I've enjoyed meeting so many people since my arrival. I am particularly interested in the American way of business. Last night, several of the gentlemen present were kind enough to offer me some useful insights."

Audrey nodded, understanding exactly what Gannon

was telling her beneath the overt message. She was pleased. Now she just needed to get him apart from her mother, where they could talk over his opportunities.

"Ah, business?" her mother said with distaste. "I can hardly imagine what thrall business can hold for a gentleman such as yourself."

"The world is changing, Mrs. St. Clair. I consider myself to be a man of vision. Those who can't change with the times are often left behind. I don't want to count myself among their number. I try to stay abreast of all the new thinking." Gannon leaned forward. "In fact, I must confess that was part of my reason for calling today. I had hoped to discuss some business with your husband."

Audrey watched her mother's eyes narrow ever so slightly, calculating her next move. She wasn't pleased with Gannon's answer. "Then it's a good thing, Camberly, that seeing Mr. St. Clair was only part of your reason for coming." Violet managed a light laugh that hid her disappointment. "You've missed him. He's at the Reading Room this afternoon. What was the other reason for coming?"

Audrey's gaze slid in Gannon's direction. Was he up to matching her mother's wit? She needn't have worried. Gannon reached for the square, wrapped package he'd set down. "I brought this for Miss St. Clair, with your permission, ma'am. It's a book that features Camberly Hall. A few years ago, an ambitious squire in the area made a study of the great houses in our region and put it all into this volume. The drawings of the homes are quite well done and accurate."

Violet nodded her approval, and Audrey smiled, slipping the string off the package. Gannon had scored a direct hit. Her mother's disappointment had been firmly overcome. Audrey leafed through the exquisitely-done book. "What page is Camberly Hall on, milord?"

Gannon took the opportunity to move beside her and look over her shoulder, a gesture her mother noted immediately. "Page thirty-eight," he offered. "That's drawn from the garden side. Camberly's gardens in the spring are not to be missed, although my favorite time of year is the fall, when the leaves in the Camberly woods are in full color."

There was a wistful note in Gannon's voice that caused Audrey to look up at him. "New England falls are beautiful in that way too," Audrey supplied. But with luck and if her plan worked, neither she nor Gannon would be there to see it.

The tea tray arrived, and talk turned to gardens and landscaping. Her mother guided the conversation, no doubt eager to glean more information about his estate. Audrey didn't mind. While her mother focused on the material aspects of Gannon's details, Audrey found herself focusing on the passion he conveyed for the topic. It gave her an idea for getting Gannon alone.

When tea was finished, Audrey set down her cup. "I don't pretend our gardens here can match Camberly's, but I'd be glad to show you our grounds. Perhaps it might ease the pain of being away from home a bit."

"It's a splendid idea." Her mother seconded the thought. "Do go, Camberly, and see the gardens. Make sure Audrey shows you the roses. They're particularly lovely this year."

"All right, talk quickly. Tell me everything," Audrey said the moment they stepped onto the bricked path that wound through the gardens.

"So much for a leisurely stroll," Gannon commented. "I thought I was to see the roses and relieve my homesickness."

"We can do both." Audrey tilted her head sideways to look at him with mock severity. "Besides, you knew this was just a ruse to get some time alone to discuss our progress. I can't possibly tell my mother I want to discuss business with you."

"And here I was hoping you might like me, just a little." Gannon feigned hurt feelings,

"Stop it. You know I like you. I don't go to all this effort for just anyone."

"No, I don't imagine you do go to the effort just for people who can help you get something you want." Gannon's tone turned serious. "How's our plan progressing on your end?"

They stopped walking, having reached a stone wall that marked the end of the St. Clair property, separating it from a heavily used walking path that wound between the great houses of Newport and the Atlantic.

"You're doing fabulously. Showing off your home in that book today was a stroke of genius, equal to Caroline Astor's brooch box. You're quite masterful when it comes to courtship rituals."

"I can be," Gannon said in a cryptic tone that caused Audrey to look at him strangely. His gaze was intent on her, and she looked away quickly. He was too handsome for his own good, and they'd both do better to remember that this was a game, only a game.

"Well, don't be too masterful. It's been a short week since our formal acquaintance, and Mother is already convinced you'll propose. We have to keep her dangling for another six weeks without committing ourselves to anything significant," Audrey cautioned.

Gannon smiled. "We'll manage. Your father and friends have offered me a chance to invest with them in a short line railroad that seems promising."

"The Hudson River Line?" Audrey asked sharply, surprised that her father would have brought that particular issue up with someone he'd just met. He'd discussed it a few times over dinner.

"Yes, I believe that was it. Do you know it?"

"Do you know what they mean to do with the railroad?" Audrey queried, wondering how much her father had disclosed to Gannon. She didn't want to be between Gannon and her father. When it came to business, Wilson

St. Clair was ruthless. But Audrey didn't want to see Gannon used as a pawn. She had not anticipated this type of development when she proposed her plan.

Gannon furrowed his brow. "This is all somewhat new to me, but I believe we're to acquire the railroad and then sell it to a larger line for enormous profit so that the larger line can expand. Yes, that's right," he said, thinking through it all out loud. "We're buying low and selling high."

Audrey smiled. "You're doing admirably. That's precisely what he and his cronies intend to do. Did you never invest in England?" Investments and stocks had been such an ongoing fixture in her life that it seemed odd that Gannon hadn't thought to seek out investment as an avenue to secure his finances earlier.

"I've invested before." Gannon leaned his elbows on the stone fence and looked out over the Atlantic, calm and blue under the summer sky. "But not like this. I've invested in cargoes and boats, of course. I've invested in canal projects. But the intent was never to invest to sell; it was more of investing to acquire. I'd receive a profit from the cargo when it returned to port and was sold. What your father proposes with the railroad is a bit different. There's no end product."

"At the end there's money. Quite a lot of it," Audrey corrected. "He must like you to offer you a place with them, and he must trust you as well. The success of the venture depends exclusively on two things: money and secrecy." Audrey gripped the stone fence, her anxiety growing. She knew enough about the railroad's situation to know that the Hudson River Line was nearly bankrupt and that shares in the railroad would shortly hit an all-time low. When that low came, her father's group would swoop in and buy up the majority of the stock so that he and his group could control the railroad. If others heard of the plan, they would definitely move to block it. Timing was everything.

Audrey gave Gannon a hard look. "You will keep his secret, won't you?" Now that the plan had become real, the risk was far larger than she'd realized. She was risking more than money.

Gannon reached for her hand where it lay on the rough stone and squeezed it. "I will keep his trust and yours. A gentleman's word is not to be doubted."

The sincerity of his gesture moved her unexpectedly. Worse, it threatened to undo her carefully steeled feelings. She'd been prepared to like Gannon Maddox since that first day on the beach but nothing more. Now, the more she saw of the diverse faces he showed the world, the more difficult it was becoming to keep her emotions detached.

"You're a surprising man, Gannon Maddox. When you're with my parents and out in society, you're sleek, urbane, confident, commanding. There's a certain aura of unassailability about you that says, 'Watch me, but don't come too close.' " Audrey turned sideways to face him straight on. "Yet when we're alone like we were on the beach, like we are now, you're completely . . ." She struggled for the word, lifting a hand to push back her hair from her face where the breeze had loosed it. "Accessible," she said firmly. "When we're together, you're very accessible." Audrey gave a short laugh at her conclusion, feeling slightly self-conscious after that. She'd probably said far too much. She regrouped. "You're a very complex man, Gannon. Are all Englishmen this complicated?"

Gannon shook his head with a laugh, turning his body sideways to face her directly as well. "I suspect only earls are, and only then because we have to be. I don't think anyone has ever spoken to me about myself so thoroughly before. It's quite a novel experience to hear oneself so entirely dissected. Are all heiresses this plain-spoken?"

Audrey felt her breath catch against her will. She didn't want to feel this attraction to him that went beyond the liking she was prepared to give him. But in this moment, all she could think was, *I want this forever, this laughing, talking, bantering with this handsome man who, for some reason, is accessible—yes, accessible—to me and me alone.* The unbidden thought struck like lightning and was gone as quickly, nothing more than a flash. Yet, like the lightning of the late-summer storms that often ravaged the coastline, it was potentially dangerous.

"I suspect I am alone in that commodity," Audrey joked, trying to regain her sanity when it came to Gannon Maddox. But his next comment unnerved her as much as his earlier one had.

"And in much else, unless I am sadly mistaken, Audrey St. Clair. You are what we'd call an 'original' in London," Gannon said softly, meeting her eyes and raising a hand to push back a strand of hair that had fallen over her face again.

The moment, the gesture, were distinctively intimate. She could not brush off the poignant hush that had fallen between them, broken only by the far-off roar of the ocean below them. She swallowed, trying not to tremble when his hand moved to softly cup her jaw. Everything seemed to happen in slowed motion. Gannon cocked his head slightly to the left, giving her a long look. *He was going to kiss her,* Audrey realized. Surely he knew he couldn't? It would ruin everything. Most of all, it would ruin her perspective. Audrey said the first thing that came to mind. "Penny for your thoughts?"

Chapter Seven

I *want to kiss you, and I shouldn't.* Gannon answered Audrey's well-timed question silently in his head. Thank goodness for the intervention. A few seconds more and he would have acted on his impulse to sweep her into his arms and kiss her senseless, an impulse he'd been fighting since he'd walked into the sitting room and seen her serenely reading in the window seat, sun filtering through the panes and catching her hair so that she appeared to him as a chocolate-haired angel.

Gannon stepped back, schooling his features into impassivity. A kiss would be anathema to her. Audrey had been very clear about that. A kiss might very well drive her away, and he needed her too much for Camberly's sake to risk creating a divide between them. Yet he couldn't believe she was entirely indifferent, regardless of her plan. Even now, when she was exerting a conscious effort to resist him, her eyes told a different story as they searched his face with stunned recognition of what they'd fleetingly seen there. Perhaps later, when she had the objectivity of distance between then and now, she'd forget what she'd seen or convince herself she was mistaken. He hoped so.

"Are the roses nearby?" Gannon asked in a neutral tone. "I want to be able to give your mother a full report." He pulled out his pocket watch and made a show of studying it. "Then I must be going. I'll want to arrange for funds for the railroad venture."

"They're over here." Audrey gestured to a side path that led to a tall, white, arched arbor. Roses climbed up the arbor's trellised sides and grew along the path in well-tended bushes. Bees buzzed happily, ignorant of the pair's approach.

The roses were lovely, well worth the visit, but Gannon watched Audrey bend toward a rich red bloom and immediately understood why Violet St. Clair had insisted on Audrey's showing off the flowers. In her pale pink afternoon gown, Audrey was the perfect complement to the lush, dark crimson roses. A painter could ask for no better setting.

Gannon thought of the herb garden at Camberly, with its mixture of soft scents—lavender and rosemary, mixed with thyme and basil. His mind's eye placed Audrey at Camberly, a long basket on her arm while she gathered herbs and flowers in his gardens. Gannon shook himself. Such thoughts were not helpful. In fact, they were quite detrimental.

"Thinking of home?" Audrey straightened and steered them toward the house, remarking on his silence.

"Thinking of your mother," Gannon responded. "I imagine if you were wearing blue, we'd be looking at the lilacs or the bluebells against the wall."

Audrey shrugged. "I won't apologize for her, and I won't say you're wrong."

Gannon shot her a sidelong look, struck by a moment's intuition. "Is that what you want with your freedom? A chance to escape all this?"

"You're very perceptive, Gannon Maddox," Audrey said quietly. "I don't want to be forty-two and have nothing more to look forward to than arranging my daughter's wedding. There should be more than that, don't you think?" Audrey sighed heavily and shook her head. "But there isn't," she said, answering her own question. "All around me, there's nothing but women who waited to come out, had a year or two of socializing, then married, established households, and spent their lives trying to marry off their children to one another in spite of all the competition to outdo each other." Audrey sighed heavily. "There's a new world out there. It doesn't have to be that way. Not for me at least."

There was desperation in her voice, not disgust, Gannon noted. She might have said more, but Wilson St. Clair appeared from the house and waved to them with a loud "Halloo! Camberly, I hear you've come to talk business."

"Duty calls," Gannon said in a low voice to Audrey. "May I see you tomorrow?"

Audrey nodded. "But it will only be for a few minutes. We're going to the Casino to do some shopping in the morning. You can see me then."

Wilson St. Clair was eager to see him and discuss the railroad. Gannon found himself swept into St. Clair's study while Audrey was left to her own devices.

Within moments, Gannon was ensconced in a deep-seated leather chair across from Wilson St. Clair's massive desk, an expensive brandy in a heavy, cut-glass tumbler in his hand. Gannon tried to pay attention to all the information St. Clair was imparting about stock dividends, but his mind kept returning to his conversation with Audrey. Now he had an idea why she wanted her freedom. But what did she think she would do with it? Had she thought beyond the immediate goal? Did she recognize how difficult it would be to live with that freedom? The choices she'd have to make?

Gannon knew. He had a few female acquaintances in London who owned their own homes and held political salons. They were widows who'd elected not to marry again. But even with one marriage behind them, society continued to look askance at them for being plainspoken and single. Still, it did occur to him that married English women had more freedom than married

American women, especially when they had the right husband.

"He's the right husband for you, Audrey," Violet St. Clair announced over dinner that night, an hour after Gannon had departed from her father's study.

Audrey stopped eating, her fork in midair. "Who's the right husband?" she asked in shock. This was the kind of talk she'd wanted to avoid all summer. What had she missed while she was lining up railroad connections for Gannon?

Her mother gave her a placating smile like the kind given to little children who needed to have something repeated to them. "The earl. Camberly, of course."

Audrey breathed easier. "We've hardly had time to get to know him." This was part of the plan. This was good.

"He's all but invited her to his home, Wilson," Violet went on, ignoring Audrey entirely as she recounted Gannon's visit. "He brought a picture book of his estate to show her," Violet said meaningfully. "We'll need to look ahead and start thinking about booking passage to England."

Wilson nodded. "I'm setting him up with a fortune to be gleaned from this Hudson River Line deal. I can't have my girl marrying a poor noble. If he lacks funds, I won't have anyone knowing it. No one will say my girl was married for her money." He beamed proudly.

Her father's pronouncement got her attention. This was bad. She'd expected her mother to react with enthusiasm, but she'd not expected the same zeal from her father. She'd counted on her father's providing some resistance, putting up obstacles that would take time—ideally, the whole summer—to overcome if at all. Mutual capitulation was not a good sign. Maybe she could have Gannon acquire an annoying habit or a nervous tic.

"I think it's all a bit precipitous," Audrey said firmly, taking a swallow of her wine to hide her anxiety. "We need to know more about him."

Violet smiled again. "You're absolutely right, my dear. We have all summer to get to know him better, but so does everyone else. I wouldn't want to see him get distracted."

Wilson jumped in, waving his fork excitedly. "It's all supply and demand, Audrey. Here, there's only the one earl to go around. We can't play too loosely with his attentions. It's not like being in England, where's there's more on hand to pick from. Just today, I was explaining supply and demand to . . ."

Audrey hid a smile. Her father would be off on that tangent for at least half an hour. Economics was his favorite topic, just as marriage was her mother's. Put the two of those subjects together, and they'd have one heck of a conversation—a conversation they didn't need her for, which was just as well.

She had a lot on her mind. On one level, the plan was going well. Gannon was poised to make his first successful investment with her father. Her parents were both distracted from suitor-hunting by the attentions Gannon was paying her. He'd definitely planted the right seeds in her mother's mind as to the seriousness of his intentions. Meanwhile, she had to assure herself and Gannon that it was all a game. His intentions were a façade, and they had to remain that way, as did her responses.

The near slipup today in the garden could have been disastrous. It proved that the attraction between them could definitely be from a source other than their mutual need to preserve their marriage-free status. When she saw him at the Casino tomorrow, she'd have to tell him to ease up on the ardent courtship. Thanks to her mother's comments, she had an idea how to do that.

Gannon was waiting for her inside the main courtyard. He was dressed in tennis whites and talking avidly with Lionel Carrington when her group arrived. Gannon's appearance could hardly appear less contrived. The racquet in his hand made it obvious he was there to play tennis. Audrey's mother would suspect nothing, yet she missed nothing. Violet immediately noted Gannon's presence and steered the little group across the immaculate lawns of the Horseshoe Piazza to greet him.

Gannon was all manners, exchanging polite conversation with her mother and the other women with her. Yes, he'd played a little tennis in England. Yes, he'd be at the Lewis ball that evening.

It wasn't good form to linger overlong with small talk,

and Audrey's mother saw to it that the conversation was done before more than five minutes passed. "We don't wish to keep you gentlemen from the courts, so we shall be off. Audrey has a fitting at Worth's for her gown for Caroline's Summer Ball."

"We don't have a court reservation until eleven-thirty," Gannon said smoothly. "Perhaps I could walk with Audrey over to Worth's? I have yet to see the famed heart of Newport fashion."

Her mother couldn't resist the chance to show off Audrey on the arm of the handsome earl to all her friends and anyone else they passed.

"Do you read everyone like a book?" Audrey asked as she and Gannon made the most of walking ahead of the group.

Gannon chuckled. "It gets easier to do over time. It's not hard to figure out what most people want and then give it to them."

"We don't have much time, so I'll be brief," Audrey said, casting a furtive glance behind her. "I need you to pay attention to other girls."

Gannon shot her a confused look. "Why? I thought the plan was to be *your* suitor."

"It is, but it looks too easy, too pat. We'll never be able to drag it out all summer if there isn't a little drama," Audrey insisted.

"Ah, I see exactly what you mean. So, I am to dance and flirt with the other girls for a bit, perhaps even settle some attentions on one or two of them, in order to keep Newport guessing as to where my attentions are fixed?"

"Exactly. Two weeks should be enough," Audrey said, feeling quite pleased with her efforts to circumvent her mother's well-laid plans.

Unfortunately, it was much easier to prescribe the needed remedy than it was to take one's medicine, Audrey soon realized. She valiantly hid a grimace that night at the Lewis ball while she watched Gannon sweep a pretty cousin of their host around the ballroom with his customary grace. Audrey uncharitably wished the girl would step on his toes, selfishly wanting Gannon to only dance that well with her. But it looked as if he danced divinely no matter whom he partnered. By the ninth dance, her mother had noticed too.

"You're losing him, Audrey." Violet St. Clair flipped open her hand-painted fan with practiced grace at Audrey's side. "He left your side after the first dance and hasn't been back since." She gave a disdainful sniff. "You're managing him poorly."

"He's not a child or a dog to be 'managed,'" Audrey shot back in a quiet voice of steel. "He's a man who is free to come and go as he pleases."

Violet turned to stare at Audrey. "Then may it please him to do more coming than going where you're concerned. He is a spectacular catch. Give him a reason to stay."

Audrey's temper escalated. "He's a poor man, Mother. Like other Englishmen, he has debts and mortgages that have to be paid. Since when has debt defined *spectacular*?"

"Since that debt came attached to a title." Violet wasn't the least intimidated by Audrey's burst of temper. Instead, she met it with equal steel, which made Audrey all the angrier. "You're a fool not to see the possibilities, Audrey."

Audrey was starting to think her mother was right, at least about the "fool" part. It had only been one night, and already she was regretting her plan. How would she ever last the agreed-upon two weeks?

Two weeks of balls and picnics had passed in agonizing slowness for Gannon, filled as they were with an endless parade of uninteresting girls and not nearly enough of Audrey St. Clair. In fact, the absence of Audrey from his circle of acquaintances was precisely the reason that breakfast at Rose Bluff was a stilted affair following the weekly Casino ball. Gannon tried to ignore the tension at the breakfast table by focusing on one of the New York papers that had been placed by his plate. He shot covert looks at Lionel and Stella. Had they fought? He had no idea of knowing what had caused this shift in the usually comfortable atmosphere. But then, the last week and a half had been nothing but a miserable blur of parties and balls.

He'd danced with so many girls, after a while they all looked the same in their pink and white dresses. Goodness knew, their small talk didn't set them apart.

He missed Audrey, even though he hadn't been entirely absent from her side during their planned hiatus. He'd danced once a night with her, making it clear to society that he had not shunned her company. He made a point to have regular conversations at the Reading Room and at Bailey's Beach with her father to keep the business connection strong. But it wasn't enough. It was plain to him that there was no one in Newport he wanted to spend time with beyond Audrey. He was eager to reclaim his position at her side.

Gannon wondered if she felt the same. He'd seen her dancing and chatting animatedly with several young men who were no doubt richer than he was. Did she miss him too? He turned the page of the paper, belatedly realizing he hadn't read anything on the prior sheet.

Stella set her coffee cup down in its saucer with a sharp clank that drew Gannon's attention. He peered over the rim of his newspaper. "Is everything all right?" He hesitated, sending an inquiring plea in Lionel's direction, but Lionel seemed as uninformed as he was as to the source of Stella's pique.

"No, everything is not all right, Camberly," Stella said sharply. "You had the St. Clair chit dangling after you practically since your arrival, and you've hardly looked in her direction these past two weeks. I've tried to hold my tongue, but after last night, I must speak out. Only one dance, and you didn't offer to take her into supper!"

Gannon set down his paper. "You're angry because I didn't spend enough time with Miss St. Clair? Weren't

you the one who told me not to make it easy on her?"
He turned to Lionel. "What's that American phrase you
like to use? 'Hard to get'?"

Stella rolled her eyes. "Yes, Gannon, play *hard* to
get, not *impossible* to get. Your credibility will take a
tumble once Wilson St. Clair runs a background check
on you and discovers what a shambles your finances are
in. You need to be entrenched with the St. Clairs before
that happens. If he likes you enough, he won't let his
wife spread the gossip all over the town. Impoverished
nobles don't get picnics thrown in their honor by Caroline Astor."

"I've never pretended to be rich," Gannon said quietly.

Stella threw her napkin onto the table in a huff. "You
had a plan, and your plan was succeeding admirably.
Then, last night, you turned your back on it. You could
have proposed, married, and been on a ship back to England at the beginning of fall with all your worries
solved, but you ignored Audrey St. Clair. That's three
weeks of work gone to waste."

"My apologies," Gannon said for lack of anything else
to say in the wake of Stella's scolding. On the surface, she
was right. But Gannon couldn't tell her what was really
going on. The thought of weathering a few more days of
Stella's discontent and Audrey's absence was daunting.
He needed a break from Newport. He'd prefer spending
the last days of Audrey's plan in absentia.

"Lionel, when you leave for New York this evening,
I'd like to join you. I have some business I need to see

to before I speak with Wilson St. Clair again." Gannon was careful not to say more about that business, although it made him feel quite awkward not to be able to discuss the Hudson River Line deal with a close friend. It was quite disconcerting to know he had too much riding on the investment to risk telling Lionel.

Gannon's breakfast table wasn't the only tense dining experience taking place up and down Bellevue Avenue that morning. In some houses, where daughters had been singled out for the earl's attention the night before, mothers plotted their next moves to take advantage of the situation. At Audrey's, the tension didn't reach them until noon, everyone having risen late due to the long night. An envelope was waiting on a silver salver next to her plate.

She reached for it and pulled out the short note. She glanced at the signature at the bottom first. "It's from Camberly," she informed the table, knowing her parents wouldn't stop staring at her until she told them. "He says he's going to New York with Mr. Carrington to see about transferring funds for Father's railroad deal. He'll call on us all when he returns." Audrey looked triumphantly at her mother. "See? The war is not lost. Camberly has not deserted us."

She could kiss Gannon for his cleverness and forethought. Well, perhaps kissing him wasn't a good idea. But the sentiment was right. She never would have calmed her mother down if Gannon had left for a few days without letting them know. Her mother would have taken it as a sign of clear desertion.

"Of course Camberly hasn't deserted us," Wilson St. Clair said, waving his fork in the air. "If he doesn't do right by our Audrey, I'll destroy him financially. He'll live to regret his railroad investment." He gave Audrey a doting smile. "If he's the one you want, he's the one you'll have."

Audrey choked on a sip of water. Here was yet another unforeseen complication in her brilliant plan. So far the "brilliant" part of her plan hadn't materialized. She was fast learning that people weren't as predictable as paper. She'd have to alert Gannon when he returned. The line they needed to walk had just gotten thinner.

Chapter Eight

Gannon had never traveled much with the exception of his annual pilgrimages to London for the Season. He was a country man at heart, loving the open spaces of his estate and the call of the land. Still, he spent a significant part of each year in London, and he knew his way around a big city.

London was no backwater but an international center from which it seemed all spokes of the world radiated. Gannon supposed he was more than a bit guilty of seeing London as the sole hub of the world. After all, any Englishman worth his salt had been brought up to see the rightness of the British motto, "Make the world England."

Even so, New York City was a marvel, hardly a provincial town full of colonial idiosyncracies. When he said as much to Lionel, Lionel had laughed, saying, "We have those too, Gannon. If you want idiosyncracies, you can go to Boston. They've got so many rules in their high society, it's just no fun to be in the club."

Lionel was proud to show off his city and gladly took Gannon everywhere. The day Lionel took him to Newspaper Row, where the major newspapers were headquartered, Gannon had to concentrate on not walking around looking up. Lionel politely let him gawk at New York Tribune Building before heading over to the GB Post Produce Exchange on their way to the financial district.

"Unbelievable!" Gannon craned his neck up at the Produce Exchange's ten stories and magnificent tower.

Lionel did his best to feign modesty at the compliment to his city. "There's more on the way. Chicago has the jump on New York just now. Chicago has taller buildings, but it won't be long before New York catches up and surpasses those inlanders."

"They're impressive buildings, but I'd hate to have an office on top. It would take me all day to get there, and I'd be too tired to work!" Gannon joked.

"We're fixing that too," Lionel said excitedly. "I am currently involved with a group of investors who are backing some experiments with personal elevators that could carry people to the upper floors in a minimal amount of time, much faster than walking it."

"Really?" Gannon took another look at the building. "Then I suppose the potential for tall buildings is unlimited."

"Well, there are limitations other than our legs," Lionel acceded. "There's the issue of structural soundness. We're working on that too, but it may take more time than the elevator."

"Are all American cities like this one?" Gannon asked as they continued to progress down the street. "I imagine the capital is."

Lionel snorted. "Hardly. Philadelphia and Washington have seen their heyday. Well, at least Philadelphia has. I am not sure Washington ever had one. Even during the War Between the States, DC was nothing more than muddy roads and tent cities."

They arrived at the bank and went inside, Lionel leaving Gannon in the capable hands of the vice president, who was thrilled to be of assistance to a real-life earl.

There was more sightseeing that afternoon and dinner at Delmonico's Restaurant, which Lionel insisted made any visit to Manhattan complete.

"So, honestly, Gannon, what do you think of our sleepy little burg?" Lionel asked over oysters and platters of Delmonico's signature steaks.

Gannon was thoughtful for a moment. "This world of the 'new' city is quite beyond me. I understand and appreciate invention in all its guises, but give me a machine that can plow a field faster or harvest crops quicker any day. No, I'm a farmer at heart. But this all reminds me of Andrew. He likes to build things. He would love to see this, to be part of this while it's still new."

Lionel nodded, sipping ice-cold Champagne. "If you

want some advice, send him on a Grand Tour, let him see all the great architecture of Europe. Have him study in Italy. Then send him over here. There'll be a place for him with me when he's ready. There are architects all over the city looking for quality apprentices with fresh perspectives."

"I am humbled by your generosity." Gannon smiled at his American friend.

Lionel leaned over the table and said in quieter tones, "Then let me continue with my generosity." It was meant humorously but carried an edge of caution. "There will always be a place for you with me. I will always be indebted to you for the service you rendered me and Stella in England." He paused, letting their history hover between them. Gannon knew the event to which he referred. A member of Lionel's shipping company had tried to embezzle several hundred thousand dollars from the firm. In the process, Stella had been kidnapped and placed in serious danger.

Gannon waved it away. "You've more than paid for it by letting me come here with you, stay at your home, and be underfoot for an entire summer."

"No, my friend, you will not dismiss it so easily. You saved my company and perhaps my wife's life with your efforts. And by doing so, you saved mine. I did not understand that you would want to invest when you came over, so I did not offer any opportunity. Now you've thought to throw your lot in with St. Clair on some deal I don't pretend to know anything about. It's always secretive with him, some buyout or other. You don't need to do that. You're welcome to invest with my group."

Gannon was nearly guilted into spilling the plans St. Clair had for the short line railroad. "I appreciate the offer. But I need St. Clair's investment option. For me, it's the way I need to go." He lowered his voice. "I need cash, and there's the promise of a lot of it in a very short time," Gannon said meaningfully. He could tell Lionel that much at least.

Lionel gave a sad smile. "Well, I hope it works out, for your sake. Be careful. Wilson St. Clair will not look kindly on a man who jilts his daughter. He's the type of man who would blow a business deal for revenge, and he's got the millions behind him to easily cover his losses," Lionel cautioned.

To his credit, Lionel didn't press the matter again over the next two days they spent in New York. By Friday, Gannon was glad to see their private stateroom on the Fall River boat. He told himself he was eager to get back to Newport because the city had been so hot, with a humid, sticky heat. He was tired of feeling perpetually dirty from the constant presence of sweat. He and Lionel joked about how much they were looking forward to the large bathtubs and bathing rooms that adjoined each of the bedrooms at Rose Bluff.

But it was more than that. He wanted to see Audrey. He was desperate to see her, in fact. Lionel's warning had left him feeling unsure of himself and of her. He had made the transfer of funds, but he was doubting the wisdom of the investment. Were she and her father setting him up to fail miserably on purpose, perhaps as a joke to spite the Englishman? To teach him a subtle lesson about invading America, searching for an heiress to prop up his aging aristocracy? Or perhaps it was all just his paranoia when he contemplated the enormity of what he'd done—taken the last of the money and gambled it on St. Clair's business acumen.

When he pictured Audrey in his mind, conjured up her startling blue eyes and dark hair, he could not believe she was out to dupe him. It was nearly impossible to imagine that her forthright nature could even conceive of trickery when being outspoken served its purpose so much better. And so his mind vacillated on the return journey, leaving him sleepless in his berth while Lionel snored quietly on the other side of the room.

Gannon was on the wide back porch of Rose Bluff reading his mail and taking in the Atlantic breeze with a new appreciation when Stella found him at three-thirty the afternoon of their return from New York.

"Violet and Audrey St. Clair are here. Are you at home?"

Gannon stood up and set aside his mail. "Of course. I am always at home for Audrey St. Clair."

"Well, it's so hard to tell with you, Camberly." Stella linked her arm through his as she teased. "Half the girls in Newport think they'll be the next countess after the way you cut a swath through them before you left."

"I find that perfectly alarming," Gannon said in all seriousness while they walked.

Stella shot him a sly look. "I am sure Violet St. Clair does too, and that's why they're here."

Stella had had the St. Clairs placed in the music room at Rose Bluff, a big open room done in the French style at the back of the house so that the glass-paned French doors opened onto the porch and caught the afternoon breeze. They rose when Gannon entered the room. His first thought was that Audrey looked lovely, dressed as she was in an afternoon gown of cool blue trimmed in tiny white lace. Indeed, it was nearly impossible to concentrate on anything else. Her beauty dominated the room and his senses.

"Good afternoon, ladies. This is a pleasure." Gannon found the wherewithal to bow over Violet St. Clair's gloved hand and then Audrey's, giving her hand a secret squeeze as he did so. They all sat down while Stella poured tall, iced glasses of lemonade from an expensive crystal pitcher.

"We've come to talk about the picnic tomorrow," Violet began.

Gannon racked his brain for a clue as to what she referenced. "Is that so?" he said vaguely when it became clear that Violet was waiting for a response.

"Mrs. Astor is very kind to do such a thing for Camberly." Stella came to his rescue.

Ah, yes. He remembered now. An English-style picnic in honor of his visit. "I am looking forward to it." In reality, the only enticement the thought of a picnic held for him was Audrey's presence.

"Where's it to be held?" Stella asked, passing around a plate of lemon cookies.

"Caro has convinced the Benton farm to let us have the picnic there," Violet said casually, taking a delicate bite of the cookie.

Commandeered was more apt, Gannon thought. Caroline Astor was a woman who got her way. He could envision her taking possession of the farm with all the force of a general. The poor Bentons. Whoever they were, Gannon hoped they'd been well compensated.

"There will be games," Audrey put in. "A croquet course is being set up, as well as a badminton court."

"Do you play?" Violet asked with an innocent look in her eye that immediately put Gannon on alert. Innocence and Violet St. Clair didn't go together. Her chicanery would have equaled some of the best matchmaking mamas the *ton* had to offer.

"Yes, I play both games," Gannon offered.

"There you go, Audrey." Violet turned to her daughter. "Perhaps Camberly would partner you tomorrow."

Audrey blushed. Gannon thought it was most likely from embarrassment at her mother's overture. He knew his duty here, and he did it. "I enjoy sporting games, Miss St. Clair. It would be a pleasure to partner you if you would like." Not that doing his duty was any hardship. It worked out quite well that he'd have a reason to spend the day with Audrey.

Audrey played her part too. "I would like that very much. It is so kind of you to offer."

"Audrey is as good at badminton as she is at the piano. Have you heard her play yet?" Violet asked Gannon.

Another device. The dratted woman knew very well he hadn't heard Audrey play. In fact, he hadn't known she played at all. Gannon did his duty again, feeling sorry for Audrey, who was bristling silently beside her mother on the sofa. "Perhaps you could play for us, Miss St. Clair?" Gannon asked.

Audrey gave a brittle smile and made her way to the piano. Gannon followed under the pretense of lifting the lid for her. "We're doing brilliantly, I think," he whispered under his breath. It earned him a smile, a real smile, this time.

"She's desperate to win you back. She fears I am losing you," Audrey confided quietly.

"There's no chance of that," Gannon reassured her.

"Yes, but only you and I know that," Audrey teased quietly, settling her skirts at the bench.

"Play something nice, dear," Violet called. "Camberly, do convince her that Beethoven is unhealthy for her constitution."

Gannon raised an eyebrow at Audrey. She suppressed a laugh and launched into a quiet lieder by Schubert. By God, the woman had talent. Gannon could not recall when he'd heard the piano played so expertly and with so much feeling. He'd heard enough musicales and private performances given in wealthy London homes to know when someone was a hobbyist and when they were more. Audrey St. Clair was definitely among the latter.

Gannon quietly stood back from the piano to watch and to listen. It felt odd that he hadn't known this about Audrey, when he felt he knew her so well in spite of their short acquaintance. Such an omission was a telling reminder that while he guessed at many things about her, he only knew one thing for certain: She wanted her freedom. Hearing her play today, Gannon could start to guess why.

Chapter Nine

Gannon swung his racquet in a graceful lobbing motion, arcing the shuttlecock neatly over the net and into the back left corner of their opponents' court. The young man covering the back court made a gallant but futile effort to return the shuttlecock, landing the birdie in the webbing of the net.

"Game point!" Audrey cried a little too exuberantly to be ladylike, her hair coming loose from the thick braid that hung down her back. "We win!"

Gannon was loath to spoil her enjoyment of the victory with a reminder about propriety. It had been a hard fought battle against young Spurling, who was heir to his father's greengrocery fortune, and a rather capable Miss Van Duyesen, who was imagining herself jilted by the earl. She'd wanted to partner him and lay claim to his attentions by the merit of the one social call he'd paid her and the two dances they'd had. She'd not been pleased by Audrey's prior claim to partner him at badminton.

Gannon and Audrey shook hands with their reluctantly defeated opponents and sought out the shady canopy where her mother and friends sat, Caroline Astor among them.

"Splendid playing, Camberly," Wilson St. Clair said as they approached. "I don't suppose you sail as well as you play badminton?"

Gannon reached for nearby towel and wiped his face. "I enjoy sailing on occasion," he said modestly. It would hardly do to say that the last time he'd been boating, he'd crewed with the Prince of Wales' nephew at Cowes. He could only imagine what the gossip mill would make of that. They'd probably have him next in line for the crown.

Wilson St. Clair slapped him on the back. "There's a little race coming up—nothing serious of course. But I'd like to have you crew on my boat."

Gannon accepted with a nod. "I'd be glad."

"Hear, hear! A toast, then!" Caroline raised her glass of lemonade. "To our sportsman! Camberly is quite *accomplished*." She winked slyly at Violet.

"Speaking of sports, I believe we're due at the croquet field," Audrey put in swiftly, slipping an arm through his.

"Yes," Gannon said, "I do think young Spurling and his partner are eager for another go at us."

The rejoinder made for a good exit, but they weren't out of range before the comments started behind them.

"Audrey's got him back in line now, Violet. I am sure he won't stray again. He seems quite taken with her." Caroline's voice followed them in snatches.

"Yes, Audrey has him back. Now she just needs to bring him up to scratch," Violet said. "If she spent more time thinking about snaring Camberly than she did about Beethoven . . ."

Gannon shot a look at Audrey. She was blushing profusely. "It's awful, it's just awful," she said, clearly appalled at the comments. "I'm so embarrassed. I hope you don't think—" She broke off.

Gannon steered them behind a wide-trunked maple tree that blocked them from view. She needed a chance to collect herself. The remarks had clearly unsettled her. "It's all right. They're supposed to say those things, remember? I'd be doing a miserable job of courting you if they weren't."

Audrey leaned against the trunk of the tree and blew out a deep breath. "Is it like this for you all the time? All these women after you? Speculating about you as if you're a piece of real estate or a horse?"

Gannon laughed. "I suppose it is, but I try not to think about it in those terms." Had being with another person ever been this easy? This honest?

"Sorry," Audrey said, still out of sorts. "It just makes me so angry sometimes." She shook her head, lost in thought, her gaze going past his shoulder. "And I didn't want you to think the worst of me."

"What would the worst be?" Gannon cajoled softly.

With her eyes on him, he was becoming disconcertingly aware of their proximity, the awareness no doubt heightened by the intimate nature of their conversation.

She moved her gaze back to his face from the nebulous point beyond his shoulder and said frankly, "That I was like them; that I saw you as a prize to be won; that I concocted our little plan with every intention of trapping you into marriage."

"Such duplicity never crossed my mind," Gannon said with a shake of his head. In fact, very little was crossing his mind at the moment beyond the urge to kiss her. It was not a new urge but certainly an insistent one. One soft kiss. That was all.

His hand was moving before he realized it, the rest of his body in accord. He stepped close, a half step. His hand cradled her cheek and angled her face up toward his. His mouth came down on hers, tenderly, the sound of his name cut off by the gentle pressure of his lips on hers.

Whatever caution or protest she'd been about to utter died quickly. He felt her lean into him as he deepened the kiss. He broke the kiss softly and with great restraint. How had he ever thought one kiss would satisfy him? That one kiss would be enough? He wanted more, but out in the open of a picnic was no place to pursue such notions, with nothing more to conceal them than the wide trunk of a tree. Besides, he reminded himself, a gentleman did not pursue such notions with a lady of Audrey's caliber.

"Gannon?" Audrey whispered his name. She'd taken a step backward until her back met with the tree trunk, her face a complex study of emotions, part pleasure, part disbelief. "We shouldn't have . . ." she said.

"Why ever not? I rather liked kissing you, Audrey," Gannon replied, unwilling to let her deny their growing attraction as she had in the rose garden. He lifted a hand to push back a lock of hair from her face. "You need hair clips," he joked. "I am forever doing this for you."

"Fine, I'll get more clips," Audrey said uncomfortably. "My maid is always saying—"

Gannon pressed a finger to her lips. "Shh, Audrey. I don't want to talk about your maid or your hair. I want to kiss you again." He moved to take her into his arms.

She evaded him. "I don't think that's a good idea."

Gannon let her go, studying her. "We're attracted to each other, Audrey. Why can't we explore that?"

"It's not part of our deal," Audrey shot back, her tone strident.

"Does it matter? The deal can be amended. Why not make our courtship real, Audrey? Why not explore the possibilities of what might lie between us?" It seemed so obvious to Gannon, suddenly. Audrey was perfect for him, and she was not immune to him. She'd been eager enough for his kiss, and even she had to admit they enjoyed each other's company extremely well. Gannon found it difficult to fathom her resistance or the tears that started to well in her eyes.

"I like you too, Gannon." Audrey swiped angrily at

the tears. "But don't you see? It would ruin everything. I can't, Gannon. I just can't. As much as I'd like to fall in love with you, I can't do it. Not now."

Gannon was about protest when voices invaded their privacy, calling their names. It was Spurling and Miss Duyesen.

"Ah, there you are, Camberly. We've been waiting the croquet game on you." Spurling looked suspiciously between Gannon and Audrey. "Are you coming? Miss Duyesen and I demand satisfaction." He laughed at his attempt at humor.

What an ill-timed interruption, Gannon thought resentfully. He had a thousand questions for Audrey, starting with what the hell she had meant by, *I can't fall in love you now.* Did that mean she cared for him in spite of her fervor not to become an Englishman's wife? But that and much else would have to wait until he trounced the smug look right off Spurling's face.

Audrey watched Gannon use his mallet to send Spurling's ball flying away from the next wicket. One didn't have to be a mind reader to know that Gannon was angry. He was mad and making no attempt to hide it, although he'd better rethink venting his emotions so publicly. Spurling might start speculating as to the reasons they'd been delayed. If Spurling believed that Gannon's anger was due to being interrupted in a potentially compromising situation, such gossip would do her no good.

Gannon wasn't the only one who was angry. She was mad too, and she was mad at him. He'd done the one thing implicitly forbidden between them. He'd kissed her, when there was no possibility of anything more between them.

Worse, she'd liked it immensely. She'd wanted it to go on, all of it; the feel of his warm hand on her face, his mouth on hers, his body pressed against hers—that last had been her doing. To have him so close had been irresistible. The smell of him, the presence of him, was intoxicating, not just the sheer muscular physicality of him but the strength and comfort she was coming to associate with him.

That's why she was angry. Audrey took a whack at her own wooden croquet ball and sent it sailing through a wicket. The feelings he raised in her were causing a significant amount of self-doubt, and she didn't like that in the least. This was a most inconvenient time for doubting her choices now. For years she'd known her mind, known what her chosen course was. But Gannon's presence was starting to compete with that choice. Letting him turn their feigned summer courtship into a real one would be completely devastating. She was starting to think she wouldn't be able to resist the temptation he presented, even for Vienna.

Violet St. Clair declared the picnic a resounding success over lunch the next day on the St. Clair yacht. It was just the three of them, a rare occasion. Violet beamed a victorious smile across the table in a valiant effort to dispel the unnecessary gloom that had settled on her husband and daughter.

Audrey met the pronouncement with much squirming in her seat, her gaze drifting out over the calm ocean. Her mother's version of success hinged solely on the indisputable fact that Audrey had won back Camberly's attention. She'd talked of nothing else but Camberly's single-minded devotion at the picnic, glossing over his polite refusal to ride home with them, opting to go with the Carringtons instead.

Audrey heartily wished the conversation would head elsewhere. She cast about in her mind for another suitable topic. "Father, how is the railroad deal progressing?"

Wilson St. Clair glowered across the table. "Poorly, Aud. It is going poorly. The stock prices haven't dropped the way we'd hoped. I worry about waiting much longer to buy, but I hadn't anticipated buying at such high prices," Wilson St. Clair fumed.

Audrey's stomach had lurched at his first words. Now, an anxious knot took up residence in her stomach. Dear Lord, Gannon had put his faith in her, and she was going to be responsible for losing his money.

"Now, Aud, don't look so forlorn. Your Englishman just won't have as large a profit." Wilson leaned across the small table and patted her hand. He gave her wink. "What does it matter how much he clears on this deal? Once he marries you, he'll have all the money he can want."

As a point of reassurance, the comment fell far short. Worse, it brought the conversation back to the point she'd wanted to escape to start with.

"Absolutely," Violet chimed in. "We'll make him rich, and he'll make us titled. It will work out perfectly. Audrey, you really need to bring him up to scratch before the summer's out. It would be divine to announce your engagement at Caro's Summer Ball."

"I can't make him propose," Audrey said offhandedly.

"I'll remind him of all he stands to gain." Wilson rubbed his hands together. "That will help him along."

Audrey didn't think Gannon needed any "help along." He seemed to have things well in hand there without any encouragement from her parents. She just wished that her father's Midas touch hadn't chosen this deal to fail. She would have to tell Gannon so that he could prepare himself for the worst.

She didn't relish the thought of telling Gannon that his faith and funds had been misplaced by trusting her. Then again, if anything was going to put him off in regard to his belief that he was falling in love with her, that news should do it. It could quite possibly shatter their agreement altogether. He would have no more reason to stay at her side, and she would spend the remainder of the summer watching him pay court to another eligible girl while there was still time.

Audrey excused herself from the table and walked to the railing. She needed to think. For someone who'd only wanted to use Gannon for the sake of the game, she was feeling quite dismal with the outcome. Getting what she wanted, getting Gannon to rethink his growing infatuation, didn't make her happy when, by rights, she should have been ecstatic. She spent the rest of the coastline voyage at the rail, pondering exactly how she might break the news to Gannon.

Stella Carrington provided an excellent opportunity just two days later with an invitation to take lunch at Rose Bluff. Audrey's mother exclaimed it was the perfect accompaniment to seal the return of Camberly's affections. But Audrey could not share her mother's enthusiasm.

As she dressed in a lavender Worth afternoon gown trimmed in pale cream lace, all Audrey's thoughts were on explaining the dismal business outlook to Gannon. She hardly noticed when her maid finished pinning up her hair. By the time they reached Rose Bluff at the far end of Bellevue Avenue, Audrey was a bundle of nerves. On top of her worries about the conversation to come, this would be the first time she'd seen Gannon since their kiss.

She had no need to worry. Gannon was as urbane as ever with her mother, regaling her effortlessly with tales of his home. Stella was friendly, the food and setting of the highest quality. No one looking at them converse easily over the meal would guess anything was amiss. For all intents and purposes, the luncheon looked to be what it was supposed to be. Was she the only one aware that the luncheon was not all it seemed? She looked up from her crab salad to find Gannon's eyes on her, hot and thoughtful. He flashed her a brief smile full of promise.

He made good on that promise as soon as the etiquette of lunch allowed, rising from the table and suggesting that he take Audrey on a short tour of Rose Bluff. Stella agreed readily, saying it would give her a chance to talk with Violet.

"You must have had a lot of practice getting debutantes away from their chaperones," Audrey teased with a levity she didn't feel when they were away from Violet's intent gaze.

"I have my uses," Gannon parried easily. "Come in here. The Carringtons have generously let me use this room as my private office." Careful to leave the door open, he ushered her into an airy room done in masculine shades of dark blue and walnut wood paneling. Windows looked over the ocean. A large walnut desk sat in the bay of windows, looking handsome and strong, just like the man who used it. The desk had a pile of papers on one corner, certifying that it was more than an ornamental piece of furniture.

"What do you do in here?" Audrey asked, curious, her fingertips drifting over the polished edges of the desk's surface.

"I do my work," Gannon answered, moving to stand in the windows, his back to the room as he took in the view.

"I think I'd spend all my time watching the ocean,"

Audrey said honestly. "I'd put my chair on the other side so I could see out the windows. I think the ocean is what I like best about Newport. It's what I miss most when we're in New York." She came to the pile of papers set at one corner and idly looked at the top one.

She hadn't meant to pry, but certain words riveted her attention: lists of names with English pounds next to them. The name *Andrew* was scrawled at the bottom of the sheet that peeped out from underneath the top paper. "What's all this, Gannon?" She held the top sheet up.

Gannon turned from the windows. "As I said, it's my work." He was cool as he reached across the desk to take the paper from her. Instinctively, Audrey raised the paper out of his reach.

"What is your work, Gannon?" She met his gaze, studying him for clues. He didn't want her to see the paper.

"It's the finance sheet for Camberly," he said at last when it became clear she would not relent. "It's very private to me. I would appreciate it if you would put it back."

Audrey stepped back. "And I would appreciate it if you would explain it to me."

"As I said, it's private," Gannon insisted, starting to move around the desk, intent on retrieving the paper.

"What are you hiding?" Audrey moved backward. She scanned the paper. "Schoolmaster Almsworthy and school expenses, 240 pounds; pension to ex-gamekeeper Ballings, twelve pounds." She fell quiet, reading silently. There were salaries for pensioned workers, allowances for great-aunts, salaries for current employees, and expenditures for the manor house, as well as expenses on tenants' homes and the church in the village.

She could feel Gannon's eyes on her, but she couldn't stop. Audrey looked at the next page, full of totals for expenses, available income, and the shortfall total circled in black at the bottom. There was a paragraph of apology in what was likely Gannon's brother's hand and his signature.

"So now you know just how destitute we are," Gannon said.

Audrey set the paper down. "I suppose I do. But that's not the point. I had no idea how immense this was." She was shocked. She'd ignorantly bought into the common wisdom held by many wealthy New Yorkers and Americans regarding the "glamour" of the English country estate. But these balance sheets were not so much about glamour as they were about responsibility. And Gannon's responsibility was to people beyond his immediate family. She had not properly understood, and it made the news she had to tell him even more difficult.

"Gannon, I have to tell you something," she said slowly, taking time to gather her courage.

"I figured as much. You've been pensive since lunch. What is it, Audrey?"

"It's about Father's railroad. He says the stock prices aren't falling as low as he'd like. If he buys now, the profits won't be as great. But if he waits much longer to jump in, he might miss the opportunity to corner the market altogether." Audrey hedged. "It's not as if the money will be lost. It's just that there isn't as much of it as I'd hoped." She shook her head, miserable. "I am so sorry, Gannon." She gestured toward the pile of papers. She'd seen the totals. He couldn't lie to her and say it didn't matter. "What are you going to do?"

Gannon smiled and stepped toward her, taking her off guard. "I'm going to kiss you."

And he did. Quite thoroughly.

Chapter Ten

By the time she returned home, Audrey was still quite shaken by the direction the afternoon had taken. Gannon's kiss had left her wanting more instead of wanting less. Even though his kiss, his declaration of feelings that ran beyond friendship, were contrary to the agreement they'd struck and their personal goals, she could not dismiss them simply because they weren't relevant to her and Gannon's previously established parameters.

Oh, there was no doubt she wanted to feel different about his stolen kisses. She wanted to dismiss them and him as she had her other suitors. But Gannon was not of their ilk, and he was not so easily dismissed or forgotten. She might succeed in dismissing him if she worked hard enough, but she was highly skeptical of being able to successfully forget him.

Herr Woerner was waiting for her in the conservatory when they arrived back home, and Audrey threw all her concentration into the lesson. Her strategy was working until her mother was called out of the room for a brief moment, and Herr Woerner used the opportunity to slip an envelope into the pages of her sheet music.

"I don't pretend to know why a conservatory in Vienna would be writing to you at my address," he said, sounding a bit put out that he hadn't been included in her plans. "Nonetheless, they've sent this missive to me." He shot her a questioning glance.

There wasn't much time to explain. Her mother would be back in the room momentarily. Audrey nodded. "I've decided to go if they'll have me."

Herr Woerner nodded in return, a wealth of meaning in his nod and short statement. "You are ready if that's the course you choose."

The door opened, and Violet reentered the room, suspiciously eyeing them upon hearing the absence of piano music.

"I see how the trill should be played now," Audrey said in an overloud voice to compensate for the silence.

She was glad the lesson was nearly over. Between the curiosity at what the letter held and the confusion Gannon had wrought with his kiss, concentrating on music was a definite difficulty. At last, the lesson drew to an end, and Herr Woerner excused himself from the room with a polite bow to her mother.

Her mother left shortly afterward, going upstairs to

change for the evening entertainment. "I'll be along shortly," Audrey promised. "I need to put the music away." She quickly improvised a half truth. But it was enough to satisfy Violet.

Alone, Audrey opened the letter with trembling hands. The postmark read two weeks prior. It was now nearly the first of August. She'd waited all summer for the news. Audrey read the first line and closed her eyes with joy to savor the moment. She'd been accepted. Everything she'd worked for, planned for, was coming true.

Audrey wished she could celebrate. But her joy was hers alone. Her parents would certainly not understand. Her father might pat her on the shoulder and congratulate her on the accomplishment the acceptance represented, but he would not advocate for her actually attending the conservatory. Her mother would never understand. Her mother would, in fact, be embarrassed by what her daughter had done.

That left Gannon. Of all the people she knew, Gannon was the most likely to share her excitement. *If* he didn't feel betrayed. Gannon would put all the pieces of her scheme together and realize the part he'd played in helping her manipulate the situation to her advantage. He would see that she hadn't been all that philanthropic on his behalf. Of course, she had never hidden from him the profit she was getting.

She'd told him from the first that she wanted her freedom. She just hadn't told him what she wanted it for. No, she couldn't tell Gannon. So, that left no one. Well, she'd bear her excitement alone. Even if she'd felt she could tell Gannon of her acceptance, it would be wrong to celebrate in the wake of his disappointing news regarding the railroad. It didn't seem fair that she should have the success she'd hoped for, while his risk didn't appear to be paying off the way she'd planned.

But the fates were smiling on them that week. The railroad stock finally took the plummet in prices her father had been expecting, and his investment group was able to snatch up the majority of the stock at low prices. Firmly in charge of the direction the short line railroad would take, her father's investors were now assured of turning the huge profits they'd originally projected. Negotiations were already under way with a large railroad that needed to acquire the line in order to continue theirs.

"Are you happy?" Audrey said, clearly pleased with the news she was able to impart to Gannon as they drove through the farmlands of Newport. With the exception of her maid riding on the back of the carriage, they had the rare luxury of being alone. Audrey thought this indulgence was probably part of her mother's new strategy to get Gannon up to scratch with a proposal.

"You clearly are," Gannon said cryptically, clucking to the matched bays he'd borrowed from Lionel Carrington.

"Of course I am happy. Why shouldn't I be?" Audrey turned her head to look at him. "You should be too. We've accomplished what we set out to do. You have the money you need for Camberly, and . . ."

"And you have your freedom," Gannon said tersely.

"Although for the life of me, I can't fathom precisely what you need your freedom for," he groused moodily.

Audrey turned her gaze back to the road. She couldn't tell him what she needed her freedom for. The best she could do was to let him sulk if that was what he wanted.

Gannon pulled the buggy up to a quiet meadow and came over to help her down. The field was sprinkled with wildflowers, and Audrey picked a few as they walked. Still, Gannon said nothing.

"Are you always this peevish when you make money?" Audrey asked, unable to stand the silence any longer.

"I am lost in thought, I suppose," Gannon confessed. "I hadn't expected to hear good news on the investment. My head is swimming with ideas about how best to use the money, what to do first."

"And what else?" Audrey pressed, intuitively feeling that he was telling her only half of the truth.

"Well, here it is August. The summer has sped by in a flurry of luncheons and balls. We have what we want, as you pointed out. But that also means it's time to say good-bye, Audrey. Our agreement is at an end, and I find that I don't want to say farewell to you."

They'd come to a stream surrounded by shady trees. Gannon bent down to grab up some pebbles and toss them errantly into the rushing water.

"Now who is the one being plainspoken?" Audrey tried to jest. His confession had certainly taken her by surprise. There was a depth of meaning behind his simple declaration, and she was moved by it.

Gannon tossed another pebble. "I can give you your freedom, Audrey. Marriage is quite liberating for English women. It's not like here in America. A married Englishwoman can hold political salons and run charities that help people. Times are changing in Britain; a new age is upon us. You could become a patroness of the arts, sponsor a school. Anything you wish."

Except be a concert pianist. She was pretty sure noblemen drew the line there. "Gannon, stop. You don't have to list your assets," Audrey said. "I am touched you feel this way, truly I am. But it can't change anything. I told you from the start, I don't wish to be married to anyone."

He was withdrawing from her again. She could see it in the set of his jaw as he tossed his pebbles. She didn't want that. There were still four weeks until they had to say good-bye. She couldn't bear his stoic rejection that long. An audacious plan blossomed in her mind. They only had four weeks left. Nothing could change the quantity of time remaining to them. But she could change how that time was spent.

Gannon was throwing rocks at a knothole in a tree across the river now with a large amount of accuracy. Audrey picked up a small rock and threw it, coming close to the target, close enough to get his attention. When he turned to look at her, she said, "We can sulk away the next four weeks with remorse over things we can't change, or we can celebrate what our friendship has achieved. We can't simply start ignoring each other."

"What are you saying, Audrey? Is this another of your plans?" There was a ghost of a smile on his lips.

Boldly, Audrey stretched up to twine her arms about his neck. "I am saying we might as well enjoy each other while we can." It made sense to her in her desperate bid to get what she wanted. She was going to Vienna, and he was going back to England, free to marry whomever he wanted. Why not seize the moment and indulge, within reason, the attraction they'd fought so hard to keep in check?

"I think that's a very dangerous idea, Miss St. Clair," Gannon teased, but she noticed he didn't make an effort to disengage her arms from about his neck. "Let me get this straight. Seems while you're not the marrying kind, you are the kissing kind." His eyes laughed down at her, and it felt good to fall into their easy comaraderie again.

"Apparently so, when it comes to the earl of Camberly." She laughed with him just before he decided to test the hypothesis.

"She's refused you?" Lionel asked later that night, his blond eyebrows knitted together in consternation, his eyes latched onto Gannon's pacing form as Gannon walked the length of the Carrington library and back.

"No, not exactly," Gannon said, turning to do another lap on the perimeter of the large Persian rug.

"Then she's accepted your proposal?" Lionel said, his confusion growing.

"No, not exactly."

"It has to be one or the other." Lionel blew out a frustrated breath and took a sip of his brandy.

"No, not exactly," Gannon said for the third time. Audrey had him spinning, there was no question about it. For a woman who didn't want to marry him, she certainly exhibited a fair amount of passion when they were together. She was as honest in her ardor as she was with her plainspoken frankness. That was where the confusion existed. How could she say she didn't want to marry him and then kiss him as if their very souls were entwined? Such a juxtaposition made no sense.

Stella popped her head into the room. "Am I interrupting?"

"No," Lionel drawled lazily from his chair. "We're trying to figure out why Audrey St. Clair won't marry Gannon."

Stella fixed him with a considering look, her eyes mirroring something close to pity. "She's refused you, Camberly?"

Gannon felt ridiculously awkward. It was embarrassing discussing his love life with his friend and his friend's wife. He was a grown man, for heaven's sake. He offered the only defense he could summon. "No, not exactly."

Lionel groaned. "Stop saying that." Lionel shifted in his seat toward Stella. "She won't marry him, but she will kiss him. In fact, we were just discussing her exuberance in that area."

"That's enough, Lionel," Gannon growled.

Lionel let loose a loud laugh at his friend's distress.

"Enjoying this, are you?" As Gannon ran a hand through his hair, a small smile made a fleeting appearance at his mouth. If it wasn't happening to him, he'd find the whole situation comical too.

Stella put a hand on Lionel's shoulder. "He's just remembering what it was like when he fell in love with me." She gave her husband a warm smile.

"I seem to recall that too." Gannon grinned, ready to get a little of his own back. "He spent a week deciding how to approach you."

Lionel began to protest. "I'd heard that English women were a bit on the snobby side. I wanted to make sure I impressed you, dear."

Stella warmed to the opportunity to tease. "It took a week to come up with, 'Hello, I am the American shipper in town'?

"In my defense, I had something much better to say, something about your eyes being the color of river agates, but I was rendered speechless by your beauty up close, darling. I was lucky to get that much out."

Stella patted Lionel's sleeve affectionately. "Well, it all turned out all right in the end for us, and I am sure it will turn out for Camberly too. Here, I almost forgot.

This is what brought me up here." She handed Gannon a heavy white envelope. "A messenger brought it from Briar Cliff."

Gannon opened it. It was a check for his amount of the railroad profits. The amount would cover this year's shortfall and expenses for the following year with a little left over. Camberly would have time to get back on its feet and make adjustments.

"What is it?" Stella asked when he said nothing.

He managed a smile, trying to master the emotions set free within him at the news. "It's a check. Camberly is saved."

"Congratulations," Lionel said.

Stella moved to hug him, her face wreathed in a joyful smile. "We'll celebrate with Champagne tonight!"

Gannon accepted their good wishes. Empirically, he knew he was thrilled. Camberly was saved. The point of his mad gamble in America was achieved, even if it was by different means than he had envisioned. But in spite of the facts, true elation escaped him in the flush of his triumph. His victory was oddly empty, knowing that at the end of the summer, Audrey would not be at his side when he crossed the Atlantic and returned home.

In that moment, he knew he'd trade the check for Audrey at his side. Not because she represented an infinite source of wealth but because he loved her. She cared for him, but she loved her freedom more.

Unless he could change her mind.

He had four short weeks to do it. But Gannon was not

a man to back down from challenges of any sort. From bad harvests to poor finances, he'd overcome plenty of obstacles to make it this far. He'd wagered his fortune to save Camberly. Now he'd make one more gamble, this time with his heart.

Chapter Eleven

In the privacy of her bedchamber, Audrey sat at her white Louis XV writing desk, turning the page of her lady's calendar, a daintily flowered pink notebook of dates that she used to keep track of important reminders. Such organization was a useful habit, even if her mother had been the one to suggest it.

However, her mother might be surprised to see the kinds of things Audrey wrote down in the date book. Since March, the calendar had become a countdown to Vienna. She'd written down the application deadline in April. She'd written down speculative dates it would take the application to travel from New York to Vienna, possible dates by which a response would be likely. Since her acceptance into the conservatory, she had new dates to write down. She was expected at the school by September 20. Classes started on September 22.

It didn't leave her much time to make the necessary arrangements. Audrey blew out a steadying breath. After such a long period of waiting when it seemed as if time stood still, there was suddenly not enough time.

Today was the sixth of August. Crossing the Atlantic was a two-week affair. She needed to book passage soon. She made some notes in the margin of the page. She needed a ship that left during the first part of September, giving her enough time to complete the overland journey to Vienna. Ideally, she'd prefer a ship that docked in Amsterdam, making a shorter journey by train to Vienna. But a ship to Cherbourg, France, would do as well. Under the circumstances of such late notice, Audrey was prepared to be flexible.

There were other, more immediate considerations before she could worry about the ship's destination and what to do once she arrived in Europe. Before she could even speculate on those details, she had to find a way to book passage, and that required getting a hold of a sailing schedule and some money. It was the epitome of irony that she, an heiress, had no money of her own. She couldn't very well ask her parents for funds. They'd want to know what it was for. Neither could she ask her father for a sailing schedule. He'd want to know why she wanted it.

Audrey drummed a hand on the desk. Perhaps she could say the schedule was for Gannon, that he needed it to plan his return trip to England. She discarded the idea. It would seem odd that Gannon hadn't bought round-trip passage already. In all reality, Gannon already knew when he was returning, and he might have mentioned it in passing to her father. No, pretending it was for Gannon was too risky.

But maybe she could ask Gannon to get one for her. Maybe she could go so far as to ask Gannon to book passage for her. But then she'd have to tell him about her plan. Audrey bit her lip. Could she trust Gannon to keep her biggest secret?

Audrey flipped ahead through the pages and marked the days on which she'd prefer to sail. She flipped back, counting the weeks. Four weeks. Four weeks until she embarked on her dream. Four weeks until she and Gannon parted ways.

The prospect of leaving Gannon dimmed her excitement over Vienna. She would miss him. He'd become a good friend over the summer. They were more than merely co-conspirators. Perhaps more than friends. None of her male acquaintances had ever kissed her the way Gannon kissed her. To be honest, only Daniel Sutherland had ever tried to kiss her, and that had been a furtive peck on the cheek at a birthday party. The few suitors she'd bothered to encourage had not dared. She didn't have anything to measure Gannon's kisses against. But intuitively she doubted that any kiss, irrelevant of its source, had the power to render her so weak in the knees, or to fill her stomach with warm heat, as did his.

More than friends or not, her association with Gannon would come to an end in a few short weeks, she told herself firmly. It wasn't the right time in her life for a romantic entanglement. She would look back on her time with Gannon over the years and remember his kisses fondly.

Audrey shot a quick glance at the little clock sitting atop her desk. Eleven o'clock! She must have been daydreaming about Gannon longer than she'd thought. Gannon was supposed to be at the house at eleven-fifteen to take her and her mother shopping. She was helping Gannon pick out gifts for his family back in England. She wasn't even dressed. She was still in her dressing gown, having taken breakfast in her room in order to write in her date book.

Audrey rang for her maid and strode to her wardrobe, a room devoted entirely to her clothing and accessories. No mere carved wooden cabinet for her—such a piece of furniture would hardly begin to hold her gowns. She picked a carriage gown of lightweight blue fabric trimmed with white ribbons and lace, fresh and simple.

Her maid turned her out in record time, sweeping her hair up into a simple chignon that lay at the base of her neck beneath the wide brim of her hat. Audrey grabbed up a matching reticule and gloves and shot another glance at the clock. Eleven-forty. She wasn't too late, although her maid informed her that the Earl of Camberly had arrived punctually at eleven-fifteen and was downstairs in the front drawing room with her mother.

"Go on ahead and tell them I am coming," Audrey said, looking around for a parasol and debating whether she needed one, since she had her hat.

By the time she made her way down the hall to the main staircase, parasol in hand, Gannon and her mother had ventured out into the foyer to wait. "I'm sorry to keep you so long," Audrey called from the top of the stairs.

Gannon turned to look up at the sound of her voice, and her heart nearly stopped at the sight of him, although she couldn't figure out why. There was nothing different about his appearance. It was as immaculate and conservatively stylish as it always was; his hair, dark and sleek, his shoulders still as broad, his legs still as long, his bearing still as confident. Yet there was an aura about him when he smiled up at her that was utterly riveting. Perhaps it was only because she'd been thinking about his leaving and the recognition that they had only a few weeks together left.

"Beauty in any form is worth the wait," Gannon replied easily, offering his arm to her at the bottom of the stairs. "You look ravishing. Blue becomes you," he said quietly for her alone.

Audrey couldn't tear her gaze away from his face. Illogical thoughts of kissing those lips, of feeling his arms about her again, tumbled through her mind. Where had such images come from? She felt her cheeks heating. Would the simplest comment from him always conjure such remembrances? It was hard to look at him with such things running through her mind, and yet it was too hard to tear her gaze away.

In that moment, Audrey made an impulsive decision. If she had only four weeks left with Gannon, she would make the most of them, starting today.

The day was bright and warm. In Gannon's borrowed open carriage, Audrey snapped open her parasol, glad she'd spent the extra minutes searching for it. She sat next to her mother, and Gannon sat across from them, his back to the driver. "How old is your sister, Camberly?" her mother asked by way of small talk.

"Moira is fourteen." Gannon smiled fondly at the mention of his sister. It must bode well that a man cared so much for a younger sister as Gannon obviously cared for his.

"She's so much younger than you. Is your brother closer to your age?" Violet probed.

"No, Andrew is seventeen. My father and mother were blessed later in life. I was away at school during their early childhood, but that didn't stop us from becoming close."

"What's the difference in years, then?" Violet mused out loud. "You're what? Thirty-two, Camberly? You were in your late teens when they were born. And when did you inherit? I was under the impression you'd inherited at quite a young age."

"Mother, I hardly think discussing age is appropriate," Audrey gasped, aghast at her mother's audacity.

Did she think they were such bosom beaus with the earl now that she could invade his privacy?

"Camberly doesn't mind, do you?" Violet said to Gannon.

"Not at all," Gannon replied. "I am actually thirty-three. I did inherit quite young, at twenty-two. Andrew was barely ten when Father died, and Moira was eight."

Audrey hoped that would be the end of the inquisition. But her mother wasn't done yet. "What about your mother, Camberly? Does she live in London or on the estate?"

Audrey thought a brief shadow passed across Gannon's face. "She didn't live long after my father passed. She died two years later for no apparent reason except a broken heart."

"So you became a father figure of sorts at the age of twenty-four," Violet mused. "That's very admirable of you, Camberly."

Gannon managed a tight smile and called to the driver to pull over to the curb. Audrey breathed easier. The ride to the Casino shops had seemed interminable. She'd never noticed how long the short drive could be.

Gannon leaped down and handed her mother out first. He reached for her, and Audrey leaned close to whisper, "I am sorry. She was out of line."

Gannon kept a gentle hand under her elbow. "Don't worry about it. It's nothing."

"Nothing? Is that what you think? It will be all over

Newport by the time dessert is served this evening what a gallant fellow you are," Audrey said sardonically.

"By dinner? Shall we bet on that? If the rumor is your mother's doing, I'll wager we hear of it before we even sit down for dinner." Gannon's teasing tone was back, whatever shadow she'd imagined now banished.

"What shall we bet? Twenty pounds?"

"You can wager twenty pounds. I'll wager a kiss."

"If I win, I get twenty pounds. If you win, I'll give you a kiss. Hmmm." Audrey pretended to contemplate the wager. "All right, I accept." The prospect of kissing Gannon again sent a delicious shiver through her. Their heads were so close, she could kiss him right now if it weren't for her mother standing on the curb waiting for them. They'd already tarried by the carriage overlong.

Audrey wasn't one to enjoy shopping, not the way the other women in Newport enjoyed it. But today, she was enjoying shopping immensely. Purchasing gifts for Gannon's family was infinitely more entertaining than shopping for a never-ending procession of gowns. They strolled the length of the Casino shops, studying store windows and popping into shops that caught their attention. At one store, they purchased two sets of stereoscope slides depicting the sights of Newport and New York City for Andrew. They made a last stop at Worth's boutique, where Audrey helped Gannon select lengths of fabric for Moira and trimmings for his great-aunts. While they made their selections, Gannon regaled them with tales of his beloved great-aunts' eccentricities.

Audrey and her mother were promised for luncheon at Caroline Astor's at two o'clock. Violet tried to persuade Gannon to join them. "Caro won't mind another, especially when it's you."

But Gannon refused. "I am promised as well. I told Lionel Carrington I'd meet him at the Reading Room. I'll drop you off, though."

The idea of arriving in Gannon's carriage with Gannon himself aboard placated Violet. Audrey gave Gannon a knowing look. He smiled back. They were co-conspirators at the moment.

At the entrance to Beechwood, Gannon handed them down. "I'll look forward to the dinner and dancing at the Elms later tonight. Thank you for the help shopping."

"Are you sure you won't reconsider, Camberly?" Violet inquired one last time.

"I am certain."

"Very well, then. I see a friend I must greet. Audrey darling, don't be too long." Violet swished off, calling to a woman under the enormous shade trees.

"She's insatiable," Gannon joked lightly.

"Again, my apologies."

"No, truly, I don't mind." Gannon brought her gloved hand up to brush it lightly with his lips. "You have good parents, Audrey. I loved both of mine, and I miss them every day. Love them they way they are, and be glad you can do it."

Audrey blushed and looked away. "You're too good to be true, Gannon."

"Until tonight, Audrey." Gannon dropped her hand. "I'll be looking forward to winning the wager."

"You're mighty cocky," Audrey shot back. But it was all he had to say to ensure that the wager was all she thought about the rest of the afternoon too. She was starting to desperately wish she'd lose.

By eight o'clock that evening, her wish came true. Her mother had proclaimed Gannon's noble acts throughout lunch, careful always to mention that she'd learned all this while he escorted them shopping. After lunch, they'd made the daily parade up Bellevue Avenue in Caroline Astor's carriage, stopping to share the latest news with others. When Audrey and her parents arrived at the Elms for the supper ball, the drawing room was already abuzz with stories of the earl. By the time Gannon arrived, all those assembled were about ready to pin a medal of honor onto his chest.

"I see you've lost," Gannon whispered discreetly into her ear after a gentleman stopped by their group to inquire about Gannon's family and how much they must miss him while he was abroad.

"Yes, I do believe I have," Audrey conceded quietly, turning to face him, a little smile playing coquettishly on her lips.

"I'll look forward to collecting my reward later this evening."

The look he gave her was half flirtation and half something else that Audrey couldn't name. Whatever it was, it darkened his eyes and created such a longing in her that she didn't want to wait. She wanted to drag him out to the balcony and kiss him right then.

Dinner was torturous. To Audrey's dismay, they weren't seated anywhere near each other. The hosts had arranged to have Gannon seated next to their visiting young niece in a last-ditch effort to claim Gannon's attentions. Audrey took comfort in knowing that most of those assembled knew that Gannon's attentions were firmly fixed in her direction.

What pettiness she had fallen to when she took comfort from her own sham! Audrey took a bite of the poached salmon. Would Gannon's attentions be so assuredly fixed on her if their deal didn't demand it? The question niggled at her throughout dinner as she watched him chat with the girl. She was passably pretty, if a little on the plain side. Audrey wondered what her conversation was like. What were she and Gannon talking about at the other end of the table?

"Darling, don't stare so. People will think you're jealous, or, worse, they'll think you're worried you can't hold Camberly without a tight rein," her mother said quietly from her seat on Audrey's right side.

Audrey quickly averted her gaze. She hadn't realized she'd been staring. She took another bite of salmon and turned to the young gentleman on her left, determined to shake the intruding thoughts of Gannon's impending kiss.

At last the ballroom doors were thrown open to start the dancing. She was obliged to dance with her dinner partner, who'd turned out to be quite desultory at small talk and even worse at dancing. But Gannon was waiting for her when the first dance finished, having done his time gallantly with the Oelriches' niece.

The next dance was a waltz, and she let Gannon lead her out onto the floor, incredibly aware of his physical presence—the warmth of his hand at her back, the length of his fingers in his gloves as they gripped her own. No one she'd ever danced with danced with Gannon's grace and confidence. She wondered if that had to do with the difference in ages. Gannon was a man full grown, after all. At thirty-three, he wasn't a young beau trying to figure out adulthood and all its tenets. Gannon was a seasoned man with experiences to guide him.

"What are you thinking?" Gannon said, sweeping them through a turn.

"I am thinking how the women in London must flock to you," she said honestly.

"Well, some do," Gannon replied modestly.

Audrey laughed at his humble response. "Dance me outside, Gannon Maddox."

Gannon swung them through the open French doors and out into the gardens. Unlike English town houses, where ballrooms were on the second floor after a long climb up a curved staircase, these American mansions featured wide-open ballrooms on the lower floor so that the doors exited onto wide verandahs and gardens.

The gardens were well lit enough and as yet still unpopulated by guests, since the dancing had just begun. Feeling bold, Audrey drew Gannon down the shallow steps and onto a winding path. Strains of the waltz filtered out from the ballroom into the evening. "Dance with me here, Gannon."

"Audrey, we must have a care," Gannon warned, but he was smiling at her, his eyes sparkling with the fun and mischief of their escapade. Audrey reveled in the power of his arms as he stepped them into the dance.

They dipped and swayed over the brick pathways in time to the music inside. Audrey's slipper caught on a loose brick, and she stumbled, only to be immediately righted by Gannon's sure-footedness.

The music faded, and Audrey collapsed against him, breathless. It seemed more natural than stepping away. They were both laughing. Audrey looked up into the night. "The stars are coming out," she said, raising an arm upward.

"Shall we wish on them?" Gannon asked softly, his hands riding gently at her waist, their bodies close.

"No, I don't dare trust my luck," Audrey said. "I made a wish earlier today, and it came true."

Gannon arched his eyebrows in inquiry. "What did you wish for?"

Audrey gave him a playful smile. "I wished I'd lose the bet."

"Why is that?" Gannon pressed, teasing.

"Can't you guess?" Audrey said, suddenly embarrassed by her confession. "Surely I don't need to spell it out for you."

"At last, I've managed to embarrass the outspoken Miss St. Clair." Gannon chuckled. "No, don't tell me why you wished to lose the bet. Let me believe it was because you wanted me to kiss you again. It will do my man's ego good."

Just like that, her embarrassment evaporated. Her confidence restored, Audrey pushed forward, her arms moving around his neck. "So will you? Kiss me, that is?"

"Absolutely." He dipped his head and obliged.

Audrey sank into the kiss, her mouth opening to his. Her hands found their way into the darkness of his hair. The kiss deepened, and she instinctively pressed her body into his, feeling the muscles and manly planes of him.

"Audrey, careful," Gannon murmured between what had gone from one kiss to a series of kisses. "Whatever would your mother say?"

A firm clearing of a throat brought the moment to an abrupt halt. Audrey looked past Gannon's shoulder with unfeigned horror. The object of Gannon's remark stood on the garden path, tapping her foot ominously on the bricks. "She would say, we'd better talk about your intentions, Camberly."

Chapter Twelve

Audrey stifled a gasp and would have jumped if Gannon's firm grip hadn't steadied her. "It's not what you think," Audrey said hurriedly.

"I beg to differ, dear," Violet said coolly. "It's exactly what I think it is." She managed a brittle smile. "But I have no worries. I am certain Camberly knows what needs to be done. I'll take you home, Audrey, so Camberly and your father can have a long talk."

Audrey began to protest, but a warning pressure from Gannon at her waist caused her to reconsider. "Audrey, I'll manage things," Gannon said with a quiet strength beside her.

Audrey knew she had no real choice. At least Gannon was her ally in this. Of all the people in Newport who would protect her interests, there was only Gannon. But

147

he didn't know the whole of it. He'd asked her on at least two occasions what she wanted her freedom for, and she'd neglected to give him a direct answer. She wished she had confided in him.

Gannon did not seem upset, Audrey noted, as he masterfully guided them through the ballroom to the card room where Wilson St. Clair was talking with business friends. From the moment her mother had appeared in the garden and demanded her brand of satisfaction, Gannon had efficiently taken charge of the situation, calling for the carriage and seeing to their wraps.

Audrey admired Gannon's subtle maneuverings, all of which should suggest to her mother that he would not be managed like an errant schoolboy called before the headmaster, nor would he walk back into the ballroom like a whipped cur. No one decided anything for the Earl of Camberly. He decided for himself. He alone was responsible for the turns his life took.

Unlike her. Her life evolved at the whim of others, no matter how much she railed against such machinations. Gannon handed her into the St. Clair carriage and shut the door. Impulsively, Audrey reached for Gannon's hand before the carriage pulled away from the curb. There was so much she wanted to say, but the words wouldn't come. Now that they were out of public view, hot tears threatened to overwhelm her. She wanted nothing more than to lay her head against Gannon's chest and sob out her frustrations into the black depths of his evening coat.

He squeezed her hand and pressed a swift kiss to her knuckles, his eyes holding hers. "Everything will be fine, Audrey. I promise. Get some sleep. I'll call on you in the morning."

Gannon called up to the driver and then stepped back to let the vehicle pull away down the long driveway of the Elms. Audrey fixed her gaze on him until the curve of the drive took him from her view.

"You've done well, Audrey," Violet said from her seat. "Your father and Camberly will work out the details, and we can announce the engagement tomorrow." Her voice took a sterner tone. "However, you were lucky it was I who found you two and not someone else. The results would be the same but not without the attending scandal. What were you thinking? You should have told me what you had planned."

Audrey's blood ran colder than it already was. She could feel her body start to tremble with the shock of all that had transpired. "I did not trap him," she ground out in forceful words.

Violet waved her fan negligently. "Of course not, darling. *Trap* is too strong a word for a man like Camberly. He's not a man to be *trapped*. No one coerces him into a corner without his willingness to be put there."

"It's not like that, not with him," Audrey said staunchly. But her mind roiled with a thousand thoughts at once. Did Gannon think she'd set out to compromise him? She'd certainly behaved boldly and obviously enough to create that impression.

When she looked back over the evening, her actions seemed so obvious; asking him to take her outside, to dance with her alone, and then she'd practically begged to be kissed. Seeing that kiss in her mind's eye now was mortifying; the way she'd put her hands in his hair, pressed herself up against him in what could only be considered a most unladylike manner. Only, it hadn't seemed unladylike at the time. It had seemed natural, and it had seemed mutual.

Mutual. That was even worse when she thought about their actions in the context of the conversation they'd had at the picnic. They had not talked about it since, but Gannon had not made any secret of his desire to officially change the nature of their association, to make the courting ruse real. Would Gannon look upon her actions tonight as a signal that she'd changed her mind? That she wanted to make the courtship real?

"Audrey, are you off daydreaming about your wedding already? I don't think you've heard a thing I've said." Violet's voice broke into her thoughts. "I am thinking of a November wedding. We'll still be able to get good flowers. If we press Worth for the dress before we leave for New York, it will be finished in time. If not, we'll have no choice but to put the wedding off until spring. Spring is so tricky, trying to schedule around Easter and Lent. . . ."

"He'll want to be home for the harvest. The earl can't stay until November," Audrey interrupted.

That seemed to stymy Violet for a moment. "We

could try to pull something together sooner. Oh, dear, it's already August." Violet shook her head.

Audrey didn't hear the rest of the one-sided conversation. She sank back into the seat and closed her eyes. An hour ago, life had been much simpler. It was entirely unreasonable that the price of one kiss should be so high. Well, to be honest, it wasn't just one kiss. There had been others with Gannon before tonight. And tonight hadn't been the exchange of a chaste peck on the cheek either.

For all her best intentions to avoid falling in love, she'd landed herself in the middle of her very own summer romance. It was little consolation that she'd been right—that falling in love now would be ill timed. She'd told herself that from the start. But it hadn't seemed to help. She took a modicum of comfort in her mother's words that Gannon wasn't a man to be forced into anything. But Gannon was also a man of honor and responsibility, two characteristics nobly demonstrated in his concern for his family. She could easily imagine Gannon telling her father they would not marry just as easily as she could imagine him asking permission to marry. In truth, while she knew Gannon would do what he thought was best, she didn't have a clue what that would be.

The only certainty was that tonight she'd been caught kissing the Earl of Camberly in a very intimate manner, and now she was going to pay.

Audrey was going to pay—that was the only thing that was clear to Gannon as he settled into a chair across from Wilson St. Clair in Lionel Carrington's study. Lionel offered them both snifters of brandy and folded his long form into the remaining chair.

Lionel made banal small talk with St. Clair, giving the meeting the veneer of friendliness. Gannon sipped from his glass and used the interlude to rapidly gather his thoughts. He needed a strategy, quickly. Several strategies had suggested themselves on the drive over from the Elms. All of them were viable, depending on what Audrey wanted. That was his biggest concern tonight. The sight of his confident, self-assured Audrey paling in the moonlight at the words of her mother's declaration had unnerved him.

While he would have preferred that his proposal be received under different circumstances, it was a proposal he had intended to make, with Audrey's permission. He was not disappointed at having to offer for Audrey. He had discussed his desire for them to marry with her before. But Audrey had been ambiguous in her response to that idea. In spite of that, she had kissed him intensely tonight, an equal partner in the passion that had sprung between them in the Elms' garden. Did that mean she'd changed her mind? He would not be coerced into marriage unless Audrey wanted to wed.

"Gentlemen, let's get down to business," Wilson St. Clair said during a lull in Lionel's conversation. "Camberly, you have something you want to discuss? Something that couldn't wait until morning?" Wilson cut straight to the point.

"Yes. I want to offer for Audrey." This seemed the best way to buy them some time, time to get things straightened out between them and figure out what they wanted.

Wilson St. Clair steepled his hands and studied Gannon. "Is that so? Is there a reason you need to offer for her tonight as opposed to ten o'clock tomorrow morning?"

Gannon decided Audrey got her penchant for straight talk from her father. He didn't bother to skirt the issue or to dress it up. Wilson St. Clair could ferret out a half truth with the best of them. "Your wife, sir, caught us in an embrace in the garden. For the sake of Audrey's reputation, I wanted to speak with you right away."

Gannon hoped his response sounded like that of a grown man. Still, he couldn't shake the feeling that he'd somehow been called on the carpet. No wonder a large number of his friends waited until their mid-thirties to marry. They wanted to put off the meeting with the prospective father-in-law as long as they could. He was glad Lionel was there, quiet support in the background of this conversation.

"Compromising my daughter, eh?" Wilson St. Clair eyed him with disdain. "I thought you'd be above such antics, Camberly."

There was no good answer to that. Gannon couldn't say it wasn't his idea, couldn't say that he'd warned Audrey. Such an argument would make her out to be the trollop in all this, which she wasn't. Such a statement surely wouldn't be tolerated by Wilson St. Clair. Neither could Gannon say that the fault was all his, making himself out to be a libertine, preying on the romantic sensibilities of an untried girl. That last made him want to laugh. Audrey was hardly naïve. No one took advantage of Audrey without her permission.

Gannon made the only response he could. "I am not above doing my duty, sir." There. St. Clair could read as much or as little as he wanted to into that answer.

St. Clair said nothing for a long while. Then he nodded. "Very nice, Camberly. Well said." He fell silent again, occasionally studying Gannon's face. He twirled the stem of his snifter. "Did my wife put you up to this? It can be no secret to you that she's hanging out for a title for Audrey." Wilson St. Clair sighed. "It's the one thing I can't give her."

"No, sir." Gannon's eyes blazed angrily at the thought. "I cannot be bought or bribed into such a conspiracy. I am happy to offer for Audrey, and I would have done so in the near future if not for tonight."

That raised Wilson's eyebrows, caught his attention. "Does Audrey know this?"

More awkward honesty. "No, sir. She does not. The one time I broached the subject—most subtly, I assure you—she felt this was not the right time in her life for such a commitment."

Wilson's face clouded over. "But apparently she felt it was the right time to sneak off and kiss a gentleman. Now she must pay for that misjudgment."

Gannon's eyes narrowed. It was time to assert himself,

to remind Wilson St. Clair that he was not the only man in the room with leverage. "I will not have our engagement based on the idea that Audrey must be punished for such indiscretion. Nothing need come of tonight. Only your wife saw us. If Audrey does not wish to marry me, there is no need to create a scandal."

"I can't decide, Camberly, if you say this to shirk your own responsibilities by laying the decision at Audrey's doorstep, or if you speak out of genuine concern for my daughter. Audrey's always been a little bit unconventional."

"I love her for it, sir," Gannon said sternly, with all the sincerity he could summon. "I would not willingly see her caged by a moment's indiscretion that amounts to nothing."

Wilson St. Clair spread his hands on his thighs and drew a deep breath. "Violet will have to be pacified. There's no telling what kind of difficulty she'll create."

This was an interesting turn of events. Gannon suddenly had Wilson St. Clair on the ropes, caught between his desire to appease his socially voracious wife and his desire to protect Audrey from an unwanted marriage.

Gannon knew his moment had come. He could dictate the terms. He stood up and started pacing, thinking out loud.

"Tomorrow, I will come to the house in the morning. We'll put the question to Audrey so you can hear what she has to say on the matter. In the meanwhile, you can put this proposal to Violet and to Audrey: I am happy to marry Audrey and make her the Countess of Camberly. I will marry her after her preference of an engagement, which shall be no longer than one year. We will live in England, of course, but she is free to visit New York at her leisure." Gannon paced thoughtfully for a few steps and then added, "And I will insist that she keep up her piano playing. I will support her in that pursuit with the finest instructors London can provide."

"You're very generous, Camberly," Wilson St. Clair said. "You must know Audrey quite well to know what her music is to her." Wilson gave him an appraising stare. "One wonders how one learns such things in the public nature of our social gatherings."

Gannon fixed Audrey's father with hard look. "Do not dare to impugn your daughter's virtue or my honor. I will not take kindly to further assumptions along those lines. I care deeply for Audrey, and because of that affection, I have endeavored to learn all I can about her." Behind him, Gannon heard Lionel cough a warning.

"I care for her as well. Certainly you've divined that she is my only child and the only heir to my fortune. I've heard what you can offer her. Now, I am sure you're interested to hear what kind of settlement I'll make on her once she's wed to her mother's and society's satisfaction." He said this in a pompous tone that had Gannon's hackles raised.

"I'll confer a sum of one million dollars on the two of you the day you wed. Additionally, I'll endow Audrey with her own accounts that she alone has access to in the sum of $200,000 a year. Any children you have together will be recipients of trust funds upon their coming of age. I trust you'll find this is quite the acceptable going rate on titles these days."

Gannon felt rage growing in him. Good God, the man was conferring a fortune on him. Camberly would be safe for well-managed generations. He should be leaping around the room in ecstasy. But he felt only distaste for the offer and for himself. Originally, this was the moment he'd come to Newport to achieve. He was doubly grateful to Audrey for saving him from this moment. The money they'd made on the railroad deal made it possible for him to look beyond a marriage settlement.

Gannon shook his head. "I am not offering for her because she's the richest girl in the room. I won't take a cent. I am offering for her because I have genuine affection for her."

Lionel clapped. "Well done, Gannon."

Wilson sneered at them both. "Don't be a fool, Camberly. The railroad money won't last forever, and your rotting estate will eventually have needs that extend beyond what your meager pocketbook can afford. If you won't take the money on behalf of your overinflated sense of honor, then take it for Audrey. I won't have my daughter whisked across the Atlantic to live in penury out in the countryside."

"Let Audrey decide," Gannon said sternly. "I don't

want her to think you have motivated or forced my proposal in any way. I want her to know I have offered because I wanted to offer, nothing more."

Wilson St. Clair weighed Gannon's statement. "All right. Until tomorrow. We'll expect you at ten o'clock."

Chapter Thirteen

The tension in the St. Clair library was so thick, Audrey doubted it could even be cut with a butcher's cleaver. She had spent a restless night wondering what Gannon and her father had talked about well into the early hours. Her father hadn't come home until two o'clock in the morning, and she'd heard strident voices down the hall until four. Whatever had happened, it had caused her mother and father to argue.

Over breakfast, she discovered why. Gannon had offered for her under the condition that she be willing to wed. He would not have her forced over the minor indiscretion. Her heart had thrilled to the news. Gannon had found the middle ground, a way through the tangle they found themselves in. But his proposal had put the real choice into her hands.

"You will accept him, Audrey," her mother said plainly over toast and tea. That had been Violet's mantra throughout breakfast, and it continued in the library while she paced the length of the Eastlake bookshelves.

Audrey turned a pleading gaze toward her father. He'd always been her one ally in matters like these. "Please, Father, I don't wish to marry yet. The earl is right. Only Mother saw us. We're making quite a mountain out of it all. All this can discreetly go away."

"The Carringtons know," Violet snapped. "Lionel Carrington sat in on the negotiations with your father last night."

"They would not say anything that injured the earl," Audrey insisted. "The earl's reputation is not helped by word of this getting out."

"Still, Audrey, you should not act rashly and reject him," Wilson St. Clair counseled. "Camberly is an admirable fellow. Never once did he shirk his responsibility last night. He embraced it quite thoroughly. He professed great devotion to you. He turned down my offer of a marriage settlement. Of course, that won't stop me from giving you one. I won't have you going off to live in a drafty, tumbledown English manor, even if it is a love match."

"It's not a love match. I won't marry him," Audrey protested, her cheeks hot.

But as much as she protested, Audrey could not slow the hammering of her heart when Gannon was announced and admitted to the library promptly at ten o'clock. He looked well rested in contrast to her sleepless family. He was bearing a bouquet of bright yellow flowers, which he stopped and presented to her with great aplomb, his eyes studying her face, trying to read her mind.

"Miss St. Clair, I have requested this meeting with you and your family because I have something of the utmost importance to discuss with you personally." Gannon speared her with his sharp eyes. "I have received your father's permission to ask for your hand in marriage." Gannon elegantly dropped to one knee and claimed her free hand. "Audrey, I have enjoyed your company this summer immensely, and in doing so, I have also developed a sincere affection for you. Would you do me the honor of becoming my wife and the next Countess of Camberly?"

Audrey vaguely heard her mother gasp in delight at the scene Gannon had arranged. But all her attention was riveted on Gannon's face and the expectancy in his eyes. He'd left the choice up to her, but he *wanted* her to say yes.

Panic was loosed within her. Father could have denied Gannon permission. He could have put a stop to this madness, but he hadn't. Gannon had decided to propose in front of her family, when he must surely know how much pressure there would be from her mother to accept him. Both of the people she'd counted on as allies had superficially left the decision to her, while in truth they'd decided her fate between them last night without her being in the room. Venting that anger would get her nowhere. Audrey fought to stay calm.

"Your offer is quite generous, my lord," Audrey said, amazed that her voice sounded so controlled. "Might we have some privacy, to talk? I find I want to hear more about your estate and your life in England." Her request wasn't as skillfully done as Gannon's maneuverings, but it was the best she could come up with on such short notice. At least she'd carefully avoided saying yea or nay.

"A few minutes only, Audrey," her mother said. "You can talk in the conservatory while I ring for tea."

The conservatory was not far from the library, and Audrey took the offer gladly. She firmly shut the double doors behind them, not caring what gossiping servants or her mother would think about her being alone in a closed room with a man.

"Are you all right, Audrey?" Gannon held out his arms to her the moment the door was secure, and she raced into them, burying her head against his chest.

"I can't decide if I should hate you or kiss you. Everything has become so confusing," she said. The only certainty she had right now was the solid strength of his arms.

"Hate me? I don't understand." Gannon was caught unprepared for such a statement. "I assure you, Audrey, I did everything I could to keep the situation open-ended until I could speak with you, until I knew your wishes."

Audrey looked up from Gannon's shirtfront. "But it has been decided already. Father told me you expressed

affection for me and turned down his marriage settlement. He was impressed. He's been singing your praises
all morning, and Mother's wanted this since the moment
you showed up at the Casino picnic. And you. You want
me to say yes."

"Of course I want you to say yes, Audrey. I've fallen in
love with you. I think I started falling that first day on the
beach, before I even knew who you were." Gannon
hugged her close. "I can't imagine going back to England
without you. I can't imagine the rest of my life without
you. When I do, it's nothing more than a long, bleak set
of scenes."

Now he'd done it. She was going to cry. She could
feel the hot tears forming in her eyes, and she was too
tired to hold them back. She sniffed. "That's the nicest
thing anyone has ever said to me. I am not sure I deserve
it. I'm sharp-tongued, blunt-spoken, and occasionally
unconventional. I walk barefoot on beaches, and I dance
in gardens with men I won't marry."

"Do you feel nothing for me, Audrey? Don't you enjoy our time together?" Gannon freed a hand and pulled
out a white handkerchief.

"You know I do. I just can't marry you right now."
Audrey blew her nose. He loved her. Truth be told, she
loved him. Only she wasn't nearly as brave. She
couldn't admit it. She handed the handkerchief back to
Gannon.

He pushed it away, laughing. "No, you keep it."

Audrey laughed too. It seemed an age since she'd

laughed. That was one of Gannon's many gifts. He could always find the levity in a horrible situation. He'd kept her laughing all summer.

"Just not right now? That sounds hopeful, although I must say it's not what a lovesick swain hopes to hear after declaring his love." He poked a little fun at himself, and Audrey's heart lurched. He was always so strong for her. She had to remember how difficult this must be for him. He truly did want to marry her, and she was refusing him, or at least trying to. He deserved a proper refusal with an explanation. She had to tell him. She owed him that much.

"Wait here." Audrey strode to the piano and retrieved the letter from Vienna, hidden away in the one place her mother never looked—inside the piano bench with its lifting lid.

Audrey silently handed him the envelope and watched him read.

Gannon read the envelope carefully, noting the postmark from Austria. Did she have a suitor in Europe? But no, that didn't explain the "just not right now" aspect of her near-refusal. Perhaps there was a trip she wanted to take? A girlfriend from school she wanted to visit? Audrey had mentioned that several of her girlfriends had gone abroad. He could certainly give her time for such a trip. They could visit all the girlfriends she liked on their wedding trip.

Gannon pulled out the letter on stiff white paper. There

was a seal at the top of the stationery: *The Viennese Conservatory of Music.* He shot Audrey a quick look over the edge of the paper. She was staring at him expectantly, waiting as patiently as possible—no mean feat, since patience wasn't a virtue Audrey possessed. Fortunately, he did. He had enough patience for both of them, if he could only convince her of that.

The letter was a short three paragraphs. Audrey had been accepted into a school to study piano, and a premier school at that. All the pieces of Audrey's plans fell into place. "Your parents don't know, do they?" he asked, carefully folding the letter and putting back into the envelope.

Audrey shook her head. "No."

"This is what you want your freedom for?" He'd already guessed it was. He'd heard her play.

"Yes."

"Is this why you won't marry me?" He already guessed that too, but he had to hear it from her own mouth.

"Yes."

Gannon gave a mirthless laugh. "I don't think I've ever heard such little conversation out of you before, Audrey."

"Don't be unkind, Gannon. I just shared my biggest secret with you," Audrey snapped.

"And I've shared my heart with you. I'd say that's of equal value." Gannon regretted the tone of his remark but not the reason for it. He was hurting. She'd known all along there was never a chance. He turned away and began pacing the floor.

"Gannon, I don't want to hurt you. Please don't be angry," Audrey pleaded.

"I've been your fool all summer." Gannon jammed his fists into his trouser pockets and sauntered to the bank of windows. He pulled back a gauzy curtain to look at the gloomy day outside. It mirrored his mood perfectly. It was galling to be a thirty-three-year-old man of experience and be taken in so thoroughly by a girl of twenty. She'd gulled him. How could he begin to compete with a lifelong dream?

"What do you mean? You can't mean our agreement." Audrey's anger was up. He could hear it rising in her voice. "I asked you to play the ardent suitor, and in return I'd guide a few investments for you. You got your money, and I got my freedom. I'm not to blame if you decided to fall in love with me!"

"You never told me what you needed your freedom for!" Gannon exploded.

"There was no need to. It didn't change the nature of our bargain," she said coolly.

"No, it didn't, but the nature of our kisses did!" He wanted to shake the little minx. Couldn't she see what was right in front of her? Anger warred with frustration. Gannon crossed the room to Audrey's side in three long steps and seized her roughly by the shoulders, his mouth finding hers in a bruising kiss that would not be gainsaid. But it was not a punishing kiss, and her body recognized that. After the initial onslaught, she molded herself against him, her arms about his neck, pulling him to her, as hungry and desperate as he.

Gannon pulled back. If this kiss went on much longer, he wouldn't be able to stop. "Audrey, don't deny us this." His voice was hoarse with need. "You can study piano in England. You'll have the best instructors. I won't deny you your music. You can have both. I'll buy you the finest piano available. We can have a long engagement or a short one, whatever you prefer. Just say yes." It was the best, last offer he could make. There was nothing else to give her, no other argument to make.

Something changed in her eyes. She hesitated for a moment. "A short engagement would be best, I think," Audrey said quietly. "The sooner the better."

Gannon should have heard the warning in that, but in his elation, he chose to overlook it. Audrey was his! He took her face in both his hands and offered a gentle kiss full of promise. "You've made me the happiest man alive." He kissed her again and swung her about in his arms. She smiled at his excitement.

"I suppose we should go and tell my parents," Audrey said after he'd put her down.

"Wait. Before we do that, I have something for you. I'd rather give it to you privately." Gannon reached inside his coat pocket and took out a small velvet box. He flipped open the lid to reveal a ring set with a blue sapphire. "This sapphire is part of the Camberly jewels." They were part of his entailment and could not be sold.

At the time, Gannon had been disappointed. He'd gladly have sold the gems for another harvest. Now, watching Audrey's face light up in awe of the ring, he was glad he hadn't.

He took the ring from the box and slipped it onto her hand. By luck, it fit perfectly. "A good sign." He smiled at her.

"A good sign," Audrey echoed.

Was there uncertainty in her eyes in spite of her acceptance? Gannon wanted to pretend he didn't see the fleeting doubt in her blue eyes, but his conscience wouldn't allow it. "Are you sure, Audrey?"

She met his gaze evenly. "Yes. This is all so sudden. It will take me some time to get used to the change in plans." He knew by "change of plans" that she meant the giving up of Vienna.

Gannon covered her hand with his. "I promise you, I'll make you happy," he said solemnly. He meant every word of it. Whatever misgivings she had about her decision to marry him, he would overcome every last one of them.

She squeezed his hand. "I am counting on it."

The date was set. October 4 at Grace Church in New York, with the officious Archbishop Potter scheduled to preside. Violet claimed it would give them slightly over a month upon their return to New York to settle the last details. The Newport Season had only a short three weeks to go until it was officially closed down by the Fishes' Harvest Ball at Crossways.

Violet was determined to make those three weeks into a romantic whirlwind engagement, starting with a grand announcement at Caroline Astor's Summer Ball, the highlight of the Season, occurring just two weeks after the midpoint of the summer.

Gannon would have preferred to keep the engagement quiet. He would have preferred, out of deference to Audrey, to not formally announce it. But, having snagged for her daughter the most eligible bachelor in Newport, Violet St. Clair would not be swayed.

Caroline Astor was thrilled that her ball would be the backdrop for the announcement of her dear friend's daughter's most successful engagement. She stopped at nothing to see Beechwood turned out in splendid elegance. Expensive American Beauty roses filled the Roman punch centerpiece on the refreshment table, where the best of the Astor china and silver hosted the elaborate finger foods served that evening.

What could only be described vulgarly as gallons of Champagne were on hand for the supper toast. At each supper table, guests found exquisite party favors to commemorate the occasion: elegant, painted fans from Paris with the occasion and date carefully engraved in tiny letters on the ivory handle; for the men, small silver flasks topped with a jeweled stopper, the occasion etched tastefully on one side in a silver flourish.

Gannon, Audrey, and her parents stood with Caroline Astor in the receiving line to greet the guests. Beside him, Audrey was pale and lovely in a new Worth gown of palest ocean blue trimmed in a thousand hand-sewn seed pearls to show off the deeper hues of the sapphire ring.

It had been a week since she'd accepted his proposal. The week had been filled with the business of marriage. Although Gannon was no stranger to the nature of marriages involving a peer of the realm, he'd never been quite so intimately involved in the many details of acquiring a bride. Wilson St. Clair had kept him occupied with the negotiations and contracts attaching to marrying a modern American heiress.

In the end, despite Gannon's protests, Wilson St. Clair conferred on the couple the princely sum of 1.5 million dollars in railroad stock with a guaranteed yield of five percent, or roughly 20,000 pounds sterling a year. In addition, there was an initial settlement of 500,000 American dollars. That didn't count the money St. Clair put aside for Audrey's personal use and the trust fund for the heirs. For a man who'd been pinching pence for several years, the sums were mind-boggling.

When Gannon said as much, St. Clair dismissed the largesse with a wave of his hand. "It is in accord with the current expectation. Besides, Violet says the settlement when Consuelo Vanderbilt marries Marlborough will make this one look like pennies."

Gannon stifled a laugh in the receiving line, reflecting on the conversation. The poor duke hadn't even bought a ticket to America yet, and his future was already sealed.

Audrey elbowed him. "What are you smiling at?"

"I recalled something your father said."

"I am sure my father is much more amusing than my mother," she said drolly between passing guests.

"I don't know about 'amusing,' but he's certainly as persistent," Gannon said quietly so as not to be overheard.

"I find that hard to believe." Audrey rolled her eyes, and Gannon laughed. "It's not funny. You didn't spend the week looking at swatches of white fabric. What does it matter? I can't tell the difference between a color called 'snow' and another called 'blancmange.' That's not counting all the variations of ecru and pearl. Truly, it's no laughing matter."

It wasn't, not if the hints of shadows under Audrey's eyes were evidence of the strain. Gannon reached for her hand and squeezed it in the folds of her silken skirts. "If it's any consolation, you look beautiful."

The last guest passed them with greetings, and their first duty of the evening was discharged. One benefit of being engaged was that he could keep Audrey at his side all evening. Gannon thrilled to the feel of her hand on his arm and the knowledge that it would always be there.

The orchestra struck up an opening waltz in deference to the English tradition of letting the engaged couple lead out the first dance as a waltz. Amid the applause that followed Wilson St. Clair's announcement, Gannon swept Audrey onto the dance floor. She fitted perfectly in his arms, and she waltzed with elegance, matching each step with his, but the sparkle he was used to seeing in her eyes was absent. He told himself it was just the fatigue of the engagement. He would speak to Violet himself and tell her to cut back on the planning. It was too much for Audrey.

By the time they went into supper, Gannon could not convince himself to ignore Audrey's lack of spirit, although he could tell she was trying gallantly to hide it. He waited until after the Champagne toast to pull her aside. With a gentle pressure on her arm, he guided her out to a private alcove while the others continued to eat their supper.

"Audrey, are you well?" Gannon asked once they were alone.

"Yes, of course."

"You haven't seemed yourself tonight. I am worried about you." He rather thought a happy bride-to-be would look more radiant. The brides he'd met had looked quite happy during their engagements, especially the ones marrying up.

"It's all come as such a shock. There's been so much so soon," Audrey hedged.

Gannon saw the statement for what it was. "Stop, Audrey. Don't lie to me like that. If you are uncomfortable with our arrangement, you must tell me." It cost him everything to say that.

Audrey shook her head fiercely. "No, I won't see you jilted. I saw the settlements my father drew up. That money would secure Camberly for generations. I know how much you love Camberly. I won't see you lose that because I played the fickle heart."

"And I won't have Camberly's happiness built on your own unhappiness, Audrey. Camberly will be fine. The railroad money will see it through the next few years, and by then I'll find a way to make ends meet." Gannon took both her hands in his. "Tell me the truth, Audrey. If it were just you and me, there was no title, no Camberly to save, would you still marry me?"

He knew her answer before she spoke it. Tears welled in her eyes, giving them the appearance of watery gems. "No, not this fall. I am sorry, Gannon. I can't give up my dreams."

"You're not giving them up. You're trading them for different ones, new ones," Gannon argued softly, fighting the urge to kiss away the errant tear that had started to roll down her cheek.

"I know what you've offered me. But it's not the same. I don't mean to be an excellent private pianist, Gannon. I mean to be a performer. I am certain that's not acceptable for a countess."

"I don't care. I know a few theatre patrons. I'll personally see that performances are arranged." He was begging now, and he didn't care. He was losing Audrey as surely as if she were a boat sailing out to sea and he still standing on the shore.

"Please don't, Gannon. I have to go to Vienna and try this, or I'll spend the rest of my life never knowing what I could have accomplished."

"We'll change the date of the wedding. We can marry next spring, next summer even. We can marry in June in

London, the most fashionable time of all for a wedding."
Gannon dangled every carrot he could think of. "I'll wait
for you, Audrey."

Audrey shook her head, a sad smile on her lips. "No,
it wouldn't be fair. I don't know how long this might
take."

An awkward silence filled the conversation. When it
became clear Audrey wouldn't change her mind, Gannon said, "The break will be my responsibility. I won't
have you tainted by scandal, and perhaps your parents
will be more amenable to having their brokenhearted
daughter going off to Vienna to recover."

Audrey nodded. "I would be grateful. We can do it at
the Fishes' Harvest Ball, August twenty-second. It closes
the Season."

"Very well," Gannon said stiffly. "And until then?"

"I think we'll have to act as if nothing has changed. I
hope it isn't too much to ask," Audrey said.

"Nothing is too much for your happiness." Gannon
found he meant it, even if it meant losing her. It was better this way instead of finding out five years into a re-
sentful marriage, when there was nothing to do but tough
it out. However, he rather suspected the next three weeks
would be akin to rubbing salt into a wound.

Chapter Fourteen

The following three weeks were indeed frenetic. Gannon often wondered if it truly was more hectic, more crammed full of activities, or if that was merely his perspective. But perhaps everyone was feeling a certain desperation, knowing that the luxurious Season was about to end and the idyll would be over. Back to New York, back to Paris, back to the Continent.

Not that the Newport Season was any kind of vacation. Gannon barely had a moment's peace. Now that the engagement had been announced, Wilson St. Clair took him everywhere. Only Gannon and Audrey knew the engagement was a sham, so Gannon played his part dutifully, accompanying Wilson to the Reading Room, crewing admirably on the St. Clair yacht in preparation for the cup races the last week of the Season.

At least the physical exertions of sailing took his mind briefly off the debacle with Audrey. But then evening came, and the reminders were back tenfold. Every night he squired her to a ball or entertainment, danced her around the stylish Newport dance floors, laughed with her, took countless mental pictures of her in his mind to store up against all the time that would come without her.

Soon after their private decision to cry off the engagement, Audrey had asked how he was. He'd smiled and said he was fine, that he understood perfectly the motivations for her choice, that he supported her. She had a talent she could not waste. She'd smiled broadly and hugged him. His acceptance made her happy, and so he hid his broken heart, even though he'd meant every word of his support.

Whatever free time he had, he spent it in the St. Clair's conservatory listening to Audrey practice. The St. Clairs had moved a small desk into the room for him so he could conduct his business and correspondence while not stepping away from Audrey's side. Gannon snidely wondered if that was more out of Violet's fear that Audrey would let the eligible earl slip away than it was out of generosity.

Gannon studied the curve of Audrey's shoulders from his desk in the conservatory, his mind only half on the letter he was penning to Garrett Atherton. It would be the last letter he'd send. Anything he had to say to Garrett, he would soon be able to say in person. Idly, he flipped the pages of a small desk calendar. In three weeks, he'd be home.

The cup races, a two-day affair, started tomorrow. The beginning of the end. The last week of the Season would start with the races this year and end with the traditional Harvest Ball at Crossways. He would leave for New York two days after that, take rooms at the Delmonico Hotel for a night, and sail the next day. Alone.

"You're staring," Audrey said from the piano bench.

"I'm thinking," Gannon corrected, stretching and rising from his desk.

"About what?" She rose too, meeting him at the window overlooking the garden. They'd been able to continue their companionable friendship since their decision, and Gannon cherished these quiet moments with her. He would miss this the most, having someone to talk with about whatever was on his mind.

"About going home. I'll be home in time for the harvest. It seems I've been away for ages instead of a few months. And you, Audrey. When do you leave? Have you made your arrangements?" Gannon asked quietly. For propriety's sake, the door to the room was left open.

Audrey shook her head. "I have not been able to find a sailing schedule without drawing undue suspicion. I think I'll have to rely on my father to make the arrangements at the last minute, or else it will look awkward for me to have purchased a ticket so far ahead of time."

Gannon nodded. "That makes sense. Still, come here." He drew her by the hand to his desk and opened a small drawer. "Here's a sailing schedule. It's the one I brought with me in case I needed to change my ticket." He ran a finger down the column of sailing times and gave her a sidelong grin. "I took the liberty of marking a few dates for you. Here, there's a ship sailing from New York on the tenth of September. There's one earlier, on the first, but you may need more time to convince your parents."

Audrey placed a hand over his. "I can't believe you did that for me. I know this can't be easy for you."

Gannon stiffened and withdrew his hand. "Don't, Audrey. I've given you my heart. That won't change simply because you don't want to marry me at present."

A pained look flitted across Audrey's face. "This is not easy for me either. Gannon, I—"

Wilson St. Clair made an ill-timed entrance into the room. Whatever Audrey had been about to say would be left unsaid. "My dear boy, come down and see the boat. We're ready for tomorrow. Not even Astor's yacht will catch us."

Audrey smiled gamely at Gannon. "Let me get my hat, and I'll come too."

Men had all the fun, Audrey pouted the next afternoon, sitting in the open-air carriage with her mother. The day was beautiful, blue skied and white clouded, the wind on the water perfect for racing. Gannon was out on the water, with the wind in his hair, the sun on his face, while she was stuck in the carriage wearing a hat, twirling a parasol, and viewing all the excitement through binoculars.

The races had started that morning, and those who wished to watch the yachts' progression could follow their course from the cliffs in carriages once the racers came around the bluffs. To kill time before the boats came into view, a grand picnic had been planned, but Audrey had little interest in eating. She'd kept picking up the binoculars, eager for the sight of Gannon and her father's boat. At last, a call had gone up from the picnickers that the sloops had been sighted. Everyone had piled into their carriages.

Audrey found her father's boat in a tight competition with two others at the head of the race. Proudly, the St. Clair colors flew from the rigging—green and gold—the color of money, someone had once joked. "They're tied for second with the Fishes, and the Astor yacht has a slight lead," Audrey reported, breathless. The race was close, and it was exciting. Not everyone crewed their own boats. Many of the boaters hired captains and crews for the big race, much the way horse owners hired jockeys and trainers. But Audrey's father captained his own yacht and sailed with his own crew. Today, he was holding his own against the professionals.

Through the lenses of the binoculars, Audrey searched for Gannon on board the ship. She found him at the wheel and bit her lip. He was devastatingly handsome. His white shirt billowed against the wind, sleeves rolled up, collar open at the throat. Already the sun had given

a golden cast to his face. His hair blew back from his
face, and Audrey could see every aristocratic line of his
features. He was laughing at something her father said,
and then he began turning the wheel hard.

The Astor carriage came up beside them, Caroline
proclaiming an early victory for the Astor boat. "Audrey,
I didn't know you were such an avid yachting fan," Caroline noted, exchanging a knowing smile with Violet.
Audrey blushed, prepared to take the teasing.

"I think many women would enjoy racing more if
Camberly crewed their ship." Violet laughed. "Audrey
has a handsome fiancé."

"She got the last good one. . . ." Caroline's voice
drifted off into gossip about someone's husband, who'd
turned out to be more trouble than he was worth.

Audrey turned back to the binoculars and looked for
Gannon again. He was handsome. More than that, he was
kind and caring. Single-handedly, Gannon had been setting her stereotype of the titled nobleman on its ear since
she met him. What if Caroline was right, and Gannon was
the last good one? What was she throwing away by de-
clining his offer?

Audrey chewed her lip, putting down the binoculars
as the carriage moved to a new vantage point. Gannon
was unlike anyone she'd ever met. She'd never encoun-
tered a person of privilege or rank who cared so deeply
for his people. He took his noble responsibilities seri-
ously. She remembered the night at the Casino ball
when he'd taken her outside to recover. He'd told her

how reluctant he was to marry for money but how necessary it had become. She remembered the self-loathing in his voice and his commitment to doing his part nonetheless. And then there were his kisses, sharp reminders that he was not all nobility and stuffiness but a hot-blooded man with passions that went beyond the fields and crops and bank accounts.

Oh, yes, Audrey doubted she'd ever find another person like Gannon Maddox again. Was she making the right choice? Was Vienna worth giving up Gannon? The question had plagued her in the weeks since their decision.

There was so much evidence to the contrary. The girls she knew who had married abroad had not married happily. The excitement of the engagement and the wedding had paled quickly against the realities of English living. The new brides had been wooed solely for the money they brought to empty coffers. Then they were tucked away in the country, forced to kowtow to resident family members who looked down their noses because they weren't English while their husbands went off to London to spend the fortune. That life was not for her. Even though Gannon had promised something different, she could not risk it.

Audrey picked up the binoculars again and followed the boat's progress. "We're gaining, Mother!" she cried excitedly. The finish line was in view, and her father's yacht had nearly caught the lead boat.

The carriages started pulling over atop the bluffs,

disgorging their passengers. People made their way down the long wooden staircase leading to the docks where the ships would make berth. Audrey joined them, barely able to contain her excitement.

At the docks, the judges were already set up high in a raised viewing dais. Audrey pushed forward through the crowd of onlookers. Did she imagine it, or was her father's boat ahead by the length of a prow?

Her father's boat crossed the finish a half length ahead of Astor's. Audrey ran to the edge of the dock where Gannon and her father had come ashore, flushed and excited with their victory. Gannon saw her and swept her up into his arms, kissing her soundly to the delight of the crowd.

"You did it!" Audrey cried. "I saw it all through the binoculars. You were splendid!"

"Camberly is a born sailor. Too bad he loves the land so much." Her father clapped Gannon on the back.

Audrey hugged her father too. Then she was back in Gannon's arms, looking up into his tanned face, and wishing this moment could be forever, the two of them laughing under the summer sun. A thought nagged at her. It could be forever; all she had to do was say yes.

But she didn't say it, and the last week of summer slipped away, until it was time to drive the carriage down Ocean Drive to the Southern-styled mansion of the Stuyvesant Fishes for the annual Harvest Ball.

Audrey was nervous. She fiddled with her fan, sitting

opposite her parents. She and Gannon had gone over the jilt one last time this afternoon. She had offered to shoulder the blame for the failed engagement, but Gannon had insisted the scandal fall on his shoulders as much as possible. After all, he said with a characteristically charming smile, he would sail for England and never look back.

They would give out that he'd been obliged to honor a pre-existing marriage contract involving a family friend, something arranged years ago by their fathers and only just now unearthed when Gannon's solicitors were preparing the marriage paperwork. Being a man of honor, Gannon felt he must uphold the previous contract signed by his father.

It was a good story. With luck, even Gannon would come out of it with minimal scandal. How could such honor be faulted?

The white facade of Crossways loomed, and their carriage let them out. Everyone was in high spirits, caught up in the excitement and bustle of Season's close. Tonight, Newport's high society would dance until sunrise. Tomorrow, they'd sleep late while their maids and footmen began the task of shutting down the great houses that lined the cliffs.

Tomorrow would be a difficult day. Her mother would be inconsolable, and she would have to contend with it. Gannon would be gone by late afternoon on the night ferry to New York. It was a day earlier than he'd originally planned, but she understood his need to distance himself from Newport, from her, once he'd played his part. She would face Violet's wrath alone. It was the least she could do after all Gannon had done.

Gannon was waiting for the St. Clairs under the porte cochere, offering his arm to Audrey and looking stiffly formal as they had planned. His usual charm was restrained tonight. They'd decided he had to give off the impression that something was not quite right from the start. Otherwise, his sudden need to break with her would not be believable.

He led her out for the opening Grand March and the subsequent first waltz. "I can't believe we're doing this, Audrey," he whispered through the first turn.

"Doing what? Waltzing?" she tried to tease.

The effort failed. "Calling off the engagement."

"It was never real, Gannon," Audrey reminded him, trying not to concentrate on the feel of his hand at her back, trying not to think of this as possibly the last time they'd dance together.

Gannon quirked an elegant dark eyebrow. "Never? It seemed real to me, for a few days at least."

"Yes, of course it was. I didn't mean that part, of course." Audrey covered her blunder.

"It was nice to dream for a while that you loved me, Audrey." He gave her a sad smile and quickly whipped her around the turn at the top of the ballroom.

"I do love you, Gannon." The words were out in a rush before she could hesitate and lose them.

"You do?" He looked doubtful.

"I meant to tell you the other day in the conservatory before my father came in," Audrey explained, but Gannon still looked doubtful.

"Well, maybe you do love me, just not enough." The waltz ended, and Gannon straightened his shoulders. "Shall we do it now?"

Audrey swallowed and gathered her courage. They'd plotted to do it early after the first waltz. It didn't make sense that Gannon would drag out the announcement until the middle of the evening. "Let me look at you one last time." She reached up and placed her hands on his broad shoulders, making a smoothing motion over the fabric of his coat, her heart breaking. It was for the best; Vienna called. "I wanted to remember you the way you are right now, tall and handsome," Audrey said softly right before she pulled back her hand and slapped the Earl of Camberly across the face in the middle of the ballroom.

Chapter Fifteen

Audrey buckled the last of the straps on her steamer trunk. The rest of the luggage was already in the main hall, waiting for the porter. Excitement, mixed with a sense of bittersweetness, fluttered in her stomach. She was leaving for Amsterdam at four o'clock out of New York Harbor. The intervening weeks between leaving Newport and preparing for this moment had been arduous. She'd more than earned this moment.

Her room was bare; her personal items had either been boxed up for safekeeping or packed in her luggage. Part of her couldn't believe this was happening at last. Her dream was about to start! Part of her was still trying to reconcile the happiness she felt over the impending journey with the unhappiness that had swamped her since Gannon had left. Had it been only two weeks?

It seemed an eternity since their fateful display at Crossways. Her slap had ensured that her parents came running and ushered them into a quiet salon to discuss the matter that had upset their daughter on the dance floor.

Gannon had masterfully played his part, stoically bearing the brunt of her father's initial anger over the broken engagement. She had not realized at the time that when he strode out of the salon and into the night, she'd not have a chance to see him again. He had given her a courteous, stiff good-bye befitting the occasion and simply left.

Their ruse had gone well. After a few days, her father seemed to put Gannon's choice into perspective. He even went so far as to say that Gannon was a man of honor; it was just too bad that his honor precluded the engagement. But Audrey's mother had been predictably upset. She'd wanted to call out the lawyers and force Gannon to uphold the contract he'd negotiated with Wilson. It had taken all of Wilson's patience and skill to remind her on numerous occasions that the contract clearly stated the negotiations were only legitimate if they were precluded by no other existing contracts. In this most unfortunate case, there were indeed contracts that predated this one.

Audrey had tearfully nodded her understanding and sad acceptance of the situation. The tears hadn't been feigned. She had no difficulty conjuring the demeanor suitable for a lost engagement.

She missed Gannon immensely. She'd always appreciated his wit and easy conversation. She'd come to rely on his strength and insights, his values and ethics, far more than she realized. His absence left a regrettable void that Audrey doubted could be filled by anyone or anything. Not even her music. It was the first time her music had failed to sustain her completely.

There was a knock on her door. "Miss, your parents are downstairs, and the carriages are here," a maid called.

"I'll be down in a moment," Audrey replied. She cast a last look around her room. There remained only one thing to do. She went to her writing table and opened a small drawer used for pens and ink. She pulled out a slim folder, the kind used for traveling, and opened the cover. Inside was her ticket.

The sight of the ticket made her smile. A large envelope had been waiting for her when the family returned to New York. Inside had been a short letter, nothing more than a couple of lines, from Gannon. It read simply, *Audrey, get on the ship. I bought this ticket for you in case your parents prove reluctant. I thought you'd prefer the earlier sailing date.* Underneath the sheet of paper had been a ticket that stole her breath. Even now, her breath caught at the sight of it: one first-class accommodation, White Star Line, leaving September 1, four o'clock.

Her father had purchased her a ticket, swayed by her lack of appetite and sorrowful face, but Gannon's ticket meant so much more for what it represented: his belief in her and the overwhelming reality that he'd loved her enough to give her up for her dreams.

Audrey caught sight of herself in the long pier glass. She straightened her shoulders and smoothed her cream and blue traveling suit. She looked good. She looked strong. Gannon would appreciate that. With her chin up, she stepped out of her bedroom and took the first step into her new life. She shut the door behind her and whispered to the hallway, "Thank you, Gannon."

Gannon pushed a hand through his hair, his roan hunter, Brutus, shifting beneath him as he looked out over Camberly land from a rise. Below him the wheat fields swayed in the fall wind. There was a nip in the air that reminded him summer was definitely gone. Pride swelled in his chest. This was his domain, and it was safe. He gave a critical glance to the sky. A little rain would be good. Too much rain would destroy the harvest, keeping the wheat too damp for reaping.

"You worry like a farmer." Garrett Atherton chuckled beside him, correctly noting the reason for his friend's gaze skyward.

"Too much rain means empty bellies and a long winter," Gannon said. All the money in the world couldn't control the harvest.

"It will be a much drier winter for many," Garrett said.

"That reminds me, we should go down to the village and look over the new roofs," Gannon said, turning Brutus away from the lip of the rise.

"Andrew can do it. In fact, I think he'd like to. He did a fine job while you were away," Garrett put in.

"I'd like to see them anyway," Gannon said tersely. He'd like anything that kept him busy. Since his return a few weeks ago, he'd found that the solution to missing Audrey lay in keeping busy. Fortunately, Camberly was the ideal antidote. There was always plenty to do, indoors and out.

In many ways, Camberly was acting as a balm. He was proud of the improvements Andrew had made per his instructions. He was proud of what people in the village were saying about Moira and the visits she'd paid to invalids. Even at fourteen, she'd stepped up and assumed the duties of the lady of the manor. He loved Camberly, and it felt good to be home. Garrett might laugh that he was more farmer than earl when he was home in the country, but Gannon didn't care. He rather liked it. He'd had enough of playing a part in Newport.

Would Audrey like Camberly? Was she enjoying Vienna? Was she happy playing the part she'd chosen? These were not new thoughts to Gannon. He'd gotten used to thinking them countless times a day—whenever he looked at Camberly wheat, whenever he listened to Moira's amateurish efforts at the piano. In fact, it took very little to conjure up thoughts of Audrey. Even the smallest reference would suffice.

The thoroughfare was wide enough for two horses, and Garrett had brought his horse alongside. His friend was staring queerly at him. "I told you no good could come of haring off to America," Garrett chided.

Gannon furrowed his brow. "What do you mean? I

went looking for a fortune and found it. Much good has come from the trip," he countered.

"You went looking for a wife, and I think you found a fortune and a broken heart instead," Garrett scolded.

"I seem to recall your rather pointed words about whoring myself like a common doxy. I'd think you'd be thrilled I've returned unattached and free to marry elsewhere."

Garrett snorted. "I would be thrilled if you were thrilled. Whoever she was, she gave you no less than you deserved. Still, I'd like to hear about her when you're ready to talk."

"Hear about whom?" Gannon said casually.

"Whoever it was who broke your heart," Garrett replied matter-of-factly.

December, Vienna

"Whoever it was who broke your heart did a good job," Audrey's music tutor said tersely, slapping his conducting baton against the palm of his hand.

"No one's broken my heart," Audrey retorted stiffly from the piano bench, where she'd just completed a rather sad rendition of a Schubert lieder.

"Really? I beg to differ, Fraulein. Let's try it again with a little more verve. It's a lieder, not a dirge. Soft, pastoral is appropriate; utterly melancholy is not."

Audrey launched into the piece again, making an effort to keep the feeling of the piece more upbeat. This time she succeeded, but it wasn't the first time she'd had to overcome a tendency toward melancholy.

Vienna was lively, filled with intellectual life and culture. The conservatory had lived up to all her expectations and she to its. Her marks at midterm were excellent. She loved her study of music theory and the great composers. But while Vienna seethed with life about her—dazzling parties and salons and culture—the void left by Gannon still gaped.

She'd sat down to write to Gannon on a few occasions but never sent the letters. Perhaps he wouldn't want to hear about Vienna. Perhaps it would be too hurtful, or perhaps it didn't hurt anymore. Maybe he'd moved on and relegated her to the past.

He'd said he'd wait, a voice whispered in the back of her mind. She had no business expecting him to hold to that promise. It had been an emotional time. Audrey brought the Schubert piece to a close.

"Much better, Fraulein. We're finished for the day."

Audrey breathed a sigh of relief. She needed a walk about the city to clear her head and to cheer her. She pulled on a coat and went to stroll around the park near the school. It was only two o'clock. There was plenty of time to enjoy the afternoon.

A man and woman drove past in a fashionable buggy, laughing. A child ran across her path, chasing a ball. All around her, people were together, and she was alone.

She scolded herself for wallowing so deeply in self-pity. She wasn't alone. She had her classmates. She had her music. She had the attentions of a fine patron of the arts in Vienna, Louis de Rocherer. But he didn't have hers. No one had hers. Except Gannon.

Audrey started to run, unmindful of the stares thrown her way. She wasn't sure what she meant to do. She didn't want to be sure. She didn't want to think. She ran back to her living quarters and threw a few things into a bag. She hailed a cab for the bank. She made a withdrawal and headed for the train station. She was going to England. She was going to Gannon. If he would still have her.

The Yule log gave off the heady scent of pine brought indoors, reminiscent of Camberly Christmases past. Gannon surveyed the drawing room, full of villagers and merchants alike enjoying the celebrations. Tonight, Camberly's doors were wide open to all, long trestle tables groaning with silver and food: puddings and roasts and dressings and vegetables and holiday sweets, gingerbread and mince pies.

Swags of greenery draped the enormous, man-sized mantel of the drawing room fireplace. People whirled to the steps of a country dance. Moira came to him, tugging on his hand and looking a wondrous mix of woman and child in her new blue velvet gown. He recognized its lace as some of the trimmings he'd bought with Audrey in Newport. "Brother, come dance with me. You're the only one not dancing."

Gannon could not resist her. It was Christmas Eve,

and he hadn't danced since the Harvest Ball. He let Moira lead him into the fray. People cheered at the sight of the earl among them. Gannon felt his spirits lift. He sashayed Moira up the column. He tried not to think of Audrey, he tried to keep his thoughts fixed on Moira's dancing dark eyes, but a movement beyond the phalanx of dancers caught his eye.

Chocolate hair. Great, now he was hallucinating. But the vision came again, this time with eyes that met his, the color of a robin's egg. Andrew was with her, gesturing. The vision was moving toward him. Heedless of the confusion he caused in the dance line, he moved toward it, hardly daring to believe his eyes. Audrey was here. She was dressed plainly and looked as if she'd traveled hard.

"Audrey? Is it you?"

"Gannon." She flung herself into his arms, laughing, crying. Around them, people stared. A few tut-tutted at the use of the earl's first name.

He tightened his arms about her, his joy overflowing. "What are you doing here?"

"I couldn't do it without you, Gannon," Audrey confessed, her face lighting at the sight of him. "It was all wrong without you. I am here because I can't be anywhere else. Will you still have me?"

Gannon answered her with a kiss that spoke the volumes of his soul and the depth of his devotion, while the people of Camberly cheered their approval.

Epilogue

A theatre in London, almost a year later

Audrey St. Clair, now known to her new friends better as Lady Camberly, rose from the piano bench and swept the standing audience at Royal Albert Hall a deep, gracious curtsey. The audience was generous with their rapturous applause. Tears of joy pricked Audrey's eyes as roses were thrown to the stage. She moved to gather them up, noting that many of them were American Beauties.

She'd done her best tonight, and she was proud of all that she'd accomplished. If anyone had told her little more than a year ago that she would be married to an English lord and playing in one of the most renowned performance halls in Europe, she would have denied the possibility.

But tonight was all about dreams coming true. Ten

months ago, she'd married Gannon in a quiet ceremony in Camberly's village church. Her mother would have cringed at the simplicity of the ceremony that had united them. Since then, she'd spent her time learning to become a countess and studying her music, two roles that no longer had to be mutually exclusive.

True to his word, Gannon had helped her find the instructors she needed to continue with her studies. He'd seen the town house and the country estate supplied with the finest instruments.

All those successes aside, the road to this evening hadn't been without its rough patches. In spite of Gannon's efforts, people were hesitant to embrace a female musician of her caliber. Professional music was still a man's field. Being a countess and a member of the peerage made the transition even more difficult, not easier, Audrey discovered. Nonetheless, she and Gannon had faced the social restrictions and prejudices together. Together, they'd overcome them.

Audrey waved to the crowd, acknowledging them with her bouquet of gathered roses. She beckoned offstage to where Gannon waited. She motioned him to come join her. He strode across the stage, handsome and commanding, to her side, placing a gentle kiss on her cheek. "I am so very proud of you," he whispered.

Then he turned and silenced the crowd, speaking into a relatively new sound transmitter called a microphone. "My wife, Lady Camberly, and I want to thank you all for turning out tonight. As you know from the handbills for this evening, all the proceeds from this evening's concert are dedicated to the founding of the Audrey St. Clair Musical Conservatory for Girls here in London."

The announcement was met with great applause, and Audrey was moved to tears by the emotion of the moment. Tonight was indeed special beyond words, and she had another surprise for Gannon as soon as they left the stage.

They waved once more to the audience, and Audrey let Gannon escort her to the wings, where they could be alone for a short while. The Carringtons were hosting a reception for a select few guests after the concert, and they were expected.

"Are you happy, Audrey?" Gannon asked once they were alone.

"Thrilled beyond words," she said sincerely. "Thank you for making all this possible. I doubt you knew what you were getting into when you met me on the beach."

Gannon laughed. "We started a legacy tonight, Audrey. Generations of girls will have the gift of music because of you."

Audrey smiled up at her handsome husband. "We've started another legacy too," she said mischievously. "This one, for Camberly."

She delighted in the puzzled look that crossed Gannon's face until the news registered. Then his face fractured into a wide grin.

"Not bad for a summer in Newport," he chuckled, drawing her closely against him.

She sighed, her arms about his waist. "No, not bad at all for an heiress and an earl who were both reluctant to marry."

"But not reluctant to love," Gannon corrected gently.

"Sounds like the making of a great love story." Audrey smiled.

"Yes, our story." Gannon bent to kiss her, and she gave herself over to their very own happily ever after.

POPPE   HALIW
Poppen, Nikki,
Newport summer /

ALIEF
12/12